Murder by Christmas

by

Suzanne Young

Sybown Press

Cover Designer: Karen Phillips

Sybown Press
9028 West 50th Lane, #1
Arvada, CO 80002-4441

## Dedication

This book is dedicated to
Chris and Erin,
Susanna and Chad,
Erinna and Paul,
with my love.


Other books in the Edna Davies series

Murder by Yew, 2009
Murder by Proxy, 2011
Murder by Mishap, 2012

Chapter 1

"What was your favorite Christmas tradition when you were a child?" Edna Davies asked Mary Osbourne. They were headed for the Narragansett Stop and Shop in southern Rhode Island.

"That's easy. On Christmas Eve, we'd hang our stockings on the mantelpiece and then call up the chimney to talk to 'the big elf' as my father called him. I guess it was how kids asked for things before department stores had Santas."

"Actually," Edna said, "the first department store Santa Claus dates back to eighteen-ninety in Brockton, Massachusetts. The chubby, white-bearded owner of Edgar's dressed in a red suit and walked around the store. My grandfather's father took him to Brockton on the train, just to meet the old man. Granddad said it was one of the most exciting experiences of his childhood."

Mary chuckled. "I guess that would have been fun, both the train ride and meeting Santa himself. I never got to meet Santa in person, but I always thought it was funny to see my usually-stiff mother and father bending into the fireplace and talking into the flue. I remember that was the only night in the entire winter I made sure they didn't light a fire in the living room. They tried to tell me the ashes would be cool by the time he came down the chimney, but I wasn't taking any chances." She laughed aloud before asking, "What was your favorite tradition?"

"Sing-alongs on Christmas Eve," Edna said without hesitation. "My family always gathered around the piano to sing carols. Mother played and the rest of us sang. Dad couldn't carry a tune worth a lick, but he belted out those songs as if he were the greatest opera singer alive."

The two women were laughing and exchanging memories as they left the car and went into the store.

"How about a lovely poinsettia for your Christmas party?"

Stopping her cart at a display of various sizes and colors of poinsettias immediately inside the entrance, Edna held up a healthy-looking plant. Christmas music played over the speaker system, interrupted occasionally by such requests as "Carry out at register four" or "Customer service, line one."

Rounding the table, Mary tilted her head to study the pot, her thick red hair nearly obscuring the black fleece earmuffs she wore against the biting cold of the winter morning. After a few seconds' hesitation, she straightened and shook her head. "Don't want Hank or Spot eatin' it," she said, looking around the store instead of at Edna. "Could kill 'em, ya know. I'm decoratin' with fake now that I have a dog and cat to think about."

Edna had come to know her quirky neighbor fairly well in the year and a half since the Davies had bought their retirement home next door to the Osbourne mansion. Until her mid-fifties, Mary had never had a pet and had never thought to get one. Then, last year, she'd taken in a black Labrador when the dog's owner, a childhood friend of hers, had died. Bonding quickly with "Hank" and discovering an affinity for small animals, she had also befriended an abandoned, half-grown kitten in April, naming the black feline "Ink Spot." Now, instead of living alone in the rambling, three-story house, Mary had acquired a family of sorts. Never one to go half-measures in any new venture, she frequented the library and local animal shelters in order to learn how to care for her pets.

Regarding poinsettias, Edna thought Mary was being overly cautious. "That's just an old wives' tale." When she saw Mary's lips begin to tighten into a stubborn line, she hurried to add, "Oh, I agree that your animals might get sick if they were to eat an entire plant, but you should be more concerned about decorations that contain live lilies, holly or mistletoe." Realizing she might be making matters worse in frightening Mary, Edna hastened to say, "Really, none of my children or any of the animals we've had has ever eaten a Christmas decoration, live or artificial."

She picked up one of the new variety of poinsettia, trying to decide whether to switch this year to the new hybrids that looked more like rose blossoms than the traditional pointed leaves. Her eyes passed quickly over the blue, pink and purple hues. Thinking of her home decked out in its holiday finery in years past, she had no hesitation about sticking to the old-fashioned red color. Her thoughts were interrupted before she decided on the shape of the blossoms she wanted.

"Well, looky who's here." The booming voice issued from a woman who strolled up behind Mary and bent around to peer into her face. "I recognized that red hair clear across the store." Her carrying words held the hint of a southern drawl.

The newcomer was pretty, not a great beauty, but attractive and well groomed. A red-knit tam and matching scarf complimented her dark brown hair and eyes. Her pink skin glowed with health, and she seemed full of energy and good cheer. Edna guessed her to be in her early forties. About Matthew's age, Edna thought, picturing the oldest of her four children.

Mary smiled hesitantly, "Hello, Laurel."

Edna, knowing her neighbor to have good instincts about people, mentally noted Mary's body language when she moved aside to put some space between herself and the woman. Before Edna could think much about it, though, the newcomer turned toward her and leaned over the display table.

"Laurel Taylor," she said, extending a hand and introducing herself.

Edna set down the pot she'd been holding, shook the woman's hand and returned the greeting. "Edna Davies. Pleased to meet you."

"Oh," Laurel squealed, turning to Mary, then back to Edna. "You're the neighbor. Benjy's mom."

"Benjamin," Edna corrected, narrowing her eyes at Mary before returning her gaze to Laurel. "I'm not his 'mom.' I'm his housekeeper." She smiled to take any sting out of her response.

Laurel shrieked with delight. "'His housekeeper.'

I love it. And isn't that just the way with our feline friends."

Mary glanced at Edna with a neutral expression, but Edna could see the corners of her neighbor's lips twitch ever so slightly before she said, "Laurel runs CATS, the local rescue home I told you about."

"Oh yes," Edna said, remembering one of the animal shelters in which her neighbor had developed an interest and where she volunteered when she wasn't donating her time to the South County Hospital. "I remember the name because Albert and I saw the musical on Broadway. Based on T.S. Eliot's *Old Possum's Book of Practical Cats*. We loved it."

Laurel chuckled. "I must admit the association hasn't hurt business, but tell everyone that CATS is an acronym for Cat Adoption Temporary Shelter."

"Clever of you."

"I thought so." Laurel laughed with pleasure and was about to say something else when a younger man approached the group. In his early thirties, he was close in age to the two youngest of Edna's four children, Grant and Starling. "This looks like a happy gathering," he said, stopping beside Laurel and nodding to Edna and Mary in turn. He was handsome with a rugged outdoor look about him.

"Hi, Jake," Laurel spoke with enthusiasm as she grasped his elbow with both hands and laid her cheek against his upper arm.

"Doctor Jake," Mary acknowledged with a grin, returning his nod. Nearly six feet, Jake Perry was as tall as Mary with similarly curly hair, but where her long tresses tended to frizz, his short locks waved nicely around his head. The color was darker, too, with more brown in it than Mary's carroty-red hue.

"Hello, Doctor Jake," Edna greeted Benjamin's veterinarian. "Merry Christmas." She thought he tried to loosen Laurel's grip, but the woman seemed to cling even tighter to his arm.

"Last minute shopping before the big storm hits?" he asked. "I just heard a report predicting as much as three feet. I hope all of you're ready."

"The last storm never materialized," Edna said. "If this one actually pans out, I hope it holds off until travelers get to where they're going for Christmas." She was thinking in particular of her son Grant and his family arriving from Colorado. He hadn't been back to Rhode Island for three years. When his plans to bring his family east the previous summer had to be cancelled because of his work, he'd promised everyone they'd get back for Christmas. His sister Starling had flown to Colorado both to get in some skiing and, teasingly, to escort Grant home, insuring he keep his promise.

"I'm not worried about a few feet of snow as long as everyone can make it over to my house for my Christmas Eve party," Mary piped up. "Edna and I are baking today for her family and for my party. You and Roselyn are coming, I hope."

"Wouldn't miss it."

"Neither would I," Laurel chimed in. With those words, she immediately released his arm before inquiring, "Where *is* the little woman?"

Jake took the opportunity to back away and raised his eyes to survey the crowded store. "She's around. We're picking up supplies for the clinic. That's another reason I'm keeping my eye on the weather report. Our pet photos have finally been delivered. The clinic's one big fund-raiser for the year and that online outfit who promised a four-day turnaround took three weeks. The phone lines've been so tied up with 'Where are they?' calls, we've probably lost business." He grimaced. "At least the pictures are in now, so people can come pick them up, pay us, and get their cards in the mail. Have you all been waiting for photos?" He smiled at Laurel, deepening the lines in his weather-roughened cheeks. "The money goes to help support our local animal shelters, you know."

"I've been waiting for you to bring your camera to CATS." Laurel stroked his arm, but refrained from clinging this time. "You promised me you'd be over. Remember?"

"I brought Hank and Spot to sit with Santa," Mary said when Jake hesitated in answering Laurel. "I didn't order cards, though, only an eight-by-ten."

"Benjamin doesn't like to pose for pictures. It's candid or nothing with him, so we donated instead," Edna said, wondering whether she had saved Santa Claus or her ginger cat from injury when she decided not to have a holiday picture taken.

"When can you bring Santa and your camera over to CATS," Laurel insisted, not letting the man ignore her. "I have only four in the house right now, but that's still too many for me to bring to your clinic. We *must* have a special Christmas picture taken. Can't you just imagine them draped around Saint Nicholas for a promotion photograph? We can both use it for marketing flyers, even after the holidays." She gazed up at the vet, and Edna thought the woman stopped just short of batting her eye lashes. "My kitty Christmas tree is up and all decorated. It'll make a wonderful background."

"I can spare an hour tomorrow morning," Jake said, probably aware that Laurel wasn't going to let him get away without a commitment.

"Perfect." Laurel's smile broadened. "I'll be home."

His own smile fading, Jake said, "I'd better go see what my wife is up to before she maxes out the credit card. Nice to see you ladies." As he spoke, he sidled away before quickening his step and heading farther into the store.

"I'd better be off too," Laurel said, staring after the veterinarian. "Lots to do today." She leaned across the table again, extending a hand to Edna. "You must stop in for tea sometime. I bet I could find a pretty little companion for your Benjy. My prices are the best in the area."

"Benjamin." Edna disregarded the marketing pitch. "My cat's name is Benjamin."

With a fluid motion, Laurel released Edna's hand, picked up the plant Edna had been examining earlier and turned to hurry off toward the checkout counters. Edna was too stunned to respond before the woman disappeared into the crowd. First of all, she had no intention of adopting another cat, and secondly, she had considered purchasing that particular plant herself.

Regaining her senses and her humor, she mentally shrugged. She planned to visit Schartner

Farms in the next day or two anyway where she knew they had a huge selection of healthy plants. She also wanted one of their beautifully decorated wreaths for her front door, an evergreen garland to wrap around the banister on the stairs in the front hall and, if they hadn't all been sold out by now, a six-foot Christmas tree. To Mary, she said, "Shall we get our shopping done? Time's a-wastin', as my mother used to say. Don't let me forget to pick up some candles. I forgot to put them on my list. I hope there are some of those lovely pine-scented ones left. I love the smells of Christmas, don't you?"

She talked as she merged into the flow of other incoming customers and aimed the cart toward the baking goods aisle. Mary apparently had something else on her mind. "Get to CATS early, if you plan to drink any of Laurel's tea."

Typical of Mary, she didn't say anything more until Edna prompted, "Why is that?"

"She makes a fresh pot in the morning and only adds water after that. Heats it in the microwave. If the tea gets really weak, she might add a teaspoon of leaves."

A lover of freshly brewed, strong tea, Edna shuddered at the thought. "Thanks for the warning."

Noticing the store was beginning to get busy, Edna hurried Mary along to fill the cart with flour, sugar, butter, eggs and the assortment of other baking and party items on their lists. Soon, they were heading toward the cashiers.

"I need mistletoe," Mary announced as they approached shoppers waiting at the registers.

"I saw some over by the poinsettias," Edna said.

"Would you get some for me, too? I'll get in line."

Mary returned with the mistletoe, and as they slowly moved along behind other customers, she said, "I heard Kevin Lockhorn's moved to town."

Edna frowned. She'd never heard of the man and wondered why Mary was looking at her so intently. "Who's Kevin Lockhorn?"

"Tom Greene's nephew."

Edna's stomach lurched on hearing the name of the handyman who had died tragically the previous year. Mary had introduced Tom to the Davies. He had been Mary's friend since their high school days, and it was his dog Hank whom Mary had adopted.

Edna would as soon forget she'd been the prime suspect in Tom's murder. Pushing unhappy memories to the back of her mind, she said, "As I remember, Tom's nephew was born and raised in Michigan. That's quite a move, coming to Rhode Island, isn't it?"

Mary shrugged. "I think he just got out of the army. He's gonna work for his cousin Norm. Take over the handyman business eventually, since he's Norm's only relative now."

"What about Tom's daughter and grandson?" Edna voiced the question at the same time she realized the answer. "Let me guess. Norm wouldn't think a woman capable of running a company, right?"

"That'd be my guess," Mary agreed. "He could be leadin' Kevin on. I'm thinking Norm's gonna leave the business to Danny, but it probably won't matter much. Kevin's gotta be in his mid-forties."

"And since Tom's grandson is barely six years

old," Edna said, thinking aloud, "this cousin Kevin will be close to retirement age by the time Danny's old enough to take over a business. By that time, if Norm is still alive, he'll be long retired." No great fan of Norm Wilkins, Edna snorted a laugh. "I think this is what is known as hoisted on his own petard or shooting himself in the foot. Norm is such a skinflint, he cheats his own family. He'll probably have Tom's nephew working for a song and a promise for as long as possible."

"Wouldn't surprise me a bit," Mary agreed, "but maybe Kevin knows his cousin well enough to beat him at his own game. They *are* related, after all."

Edna's stomach clenched again and bile rose in her throat as she thought of the greedy, detestable man who owned and ran Honeydew Home Repairs. About the time of Tom's death, Norm had accused his cousin and the Davies of being in cahoots to swindle the handyman company. Since then, Edna and Albert had stopped giving Norm their business and relied on young men from the nearby University of Rhode Island's Kingston campus to provide lawn and minor maintenance work, but they hadn't yet found anyone who was as skilled or as dependable or as considerate as Tom had been. Edna still missed the kind and gentle man who had become a trusted friend in the short time she'd known him.

"How's Al?" Mary's question jolted Edna back to the present. "Think he'll be up and around by Christmas?"

"Albert," Edna corrected absently and shook her head. "Even if the doctor gives him a flexible leg brace tomorrow, he's got weeks of physical therapy ahead of him."

Turning her thoughts from handymen to her husband, she felt her anxiety grow. Last month, Albert had tripped on their granite front stoop and fractured his knee cap. For the past few weeks, including the longest Thanksgiving weekend Edna had ever endured, he'd been wearing an immobilizer that extended from his ankle to the top of his leg. An active man, accustomed to being the physician instead of the patient, he had become increasingly bored and cranky since he'd been forced to sit with his leg raised and extended. She gave an inward sigh. "Catering to his needs has set me way behind in my holiday preparations. Suddenly, Christmas is less than a week away." She added in what she hoped sounded more joking than serious, "If I don't get him out from under my feet soon, one of us may not live that long."

Chapter 2

Edna dropped off Mary and the groceries at her house with a promise to be back in two hours. They would be spending the afternoon baking a variety of Christmas desserts for both households. First though, Edna needed to make lunch for Albert. She also had to have a serious talk with him about his injury and recuperation.

The cloud cover had thickened since she'd driven off earlier that morning, and she thought again of her two youngest children flying home this season. *It just won't be fair if they don't make it home this time,* she thought. Her mind drifted back over the last three years and the events that had prevented Grant from visiting Rhode Island. First, his wife Michele had died in a tragic skiing accident. Two months later, he'd remarried, and his second wife had nearly died last fall during her pregnancy. Then, they'd had to cancel their travel plans this past summer. Edna had a foreboding about this season. If her son didn't make it home … She shuddered, unable to complete the thought. As she drove around the circular, broken-shell driveway up to her front door, she pushed her unreasonable fears to the back of her mind and forced her attention on the two-story house with its weathered-gray shingles and country-blue trim.

After her husband sold his share in a medical clinic and retired, she and he spent considerable time searching for their ideal retirement home, driving from Rhode Island to South Carolina and back before finding this three-acre property in their own home state. Southern Rhode Island had everything the Davies enjoyed, from beaches to farms and woodlands. In nearby Kingston, the University of Rhode Island offered educational opportunities as well as plays and concerts, and the cultural wealth of Providence was less than an hour's drive away—close enough to take in an occasional dinner and play or concert, but far enough so Albert wouldn't be pestered by former patients stopping him on the streets to ask for "just an opinion, if you would, Doc." Albert would never second-guess another physician's diagnosis, even for someone he knew well and had treated for years.

Stepping out of the car, Edna studied the yew trees that stood sentry on either side of the front door's granite stoop. With Albert laid up, their eldest son Matthew had promised to drive down from Providence to put up the outside decorations, but had yet to do so. The house looked bare and forlorn without its holiday lights. *Five days to get ready for Christmas*, she thought with a sinking feeling and another nervous glance at the darkening sky.

As soon as she entered the front hall, Benjamin appeared from the living room to greet her. Leaning down to give the ginger cat's ears a scratch, she heard Albert call out.

"That you, Edna?"

"Yes, dear." She wondered who else he thought might have walked into the house, but refrained from asking.

"Where've you been? What took so long?"

She sighed, dreading the talk she was about to initiate. The pending, potentially unhappy conversation had put her in what, to her, was an unusually depressed mood. She enjoyed the season from Thanksgiving through Christmas. Since her children had grown and three had families of their own, this was the time of year when they were most apt to be together. A jig-saw puzzle was always in progress, games appeared, and music and laughter filled the house. Her heart lifted at the memories.

Bringing her mind back to the obstacle most immediately before her, she removed her green loden coat and matching beret with hands and arms that seemed almost too heavy to raise as she pictured her husband sitting in his recliner, imprisoned by a full-leg cast. She would probably feel more sympathetic about his plight, if she weren't so concerned about the amount of work yet to be done. She so wanted everything to be perfect for Grant's second wife who would be visiting New England for the first time. Hanging her outer clothes in the closet, she stopped in front of the hall mirror to finger-comb her gray curls into place before entering the living room. She took a deep breath to quash the sudden annoyance that jangled her nerves.

Making matters worse, Albert had a sullen look on his face. The usual twinkle in his blue eyes had been rare since the accident. His normally neat, thick white hair, badly in need of a good cut, stood up in places and stuck out above his ears. Ordinarily, he looked this disheveled only when first getting out of bed after a restless and interrupted night.

"I'm so bored, I feel like I'm going crazy."

"I know, dear," she said, trying to keep her tone light and her own frustration in check. She bent to kiss his forehead before sitting in a chair at right angles to his. Benjamin jumped into her lap where he sat staring at Albert as Edna stroked the orange fur. Chuckling inwardly and taking courage from the cat's protective stance, she began gradually, working up to her proposal.

"Thanksgiving wasn't much fun this year, was it, sweetheart?" They both knew the question was rhetorical, Albert having been put in a brace and ordered to "sit and stay" the day before family and friends were to gather. Thank goodness Matthew and Irene had already assumed responsibility for the traditional turkey dinner this year or the holiday would have been a complete disaster. As it turned out, Edna and Albert were the only ones who missed out. House-bound with her invalid husband, she refused to cook an entire turkey for the two of them and, instead, had taken clam chowder out of the freezer to heat. It was difficult to remember a more dismal day.

Albert's eyebrows drew together, his eyes narrowed and his chin lifted. Clearly, he was wondering what she was leading up to.

She bit back a smile. In more than forty years of marriage to this man, she hadn't often had to manipulate him. "With Christmas just five days away and you still unable to move about, I see we have two choices."

His eyebrows rose in silent question.

She went on. "I can sit here and keep you entertained, or I can get the house ready for us to celebrate Christmas with our children and grandchildren." This time, she waited for him to reply as she gently stroked Benjamin's back.

"What do you have to do?" he asked. The tone of his question along with the scowl on his face told her that he didn't understand all that was required to prepare for a major family holiday.

"For one thing, there's the house to clean," she began.

He interrupted. "Housekeeper Helpers come every week. The house is clean enough."

"Beds to make …"

He interjected again, "Beverly and Junie can do that when they come to clean."

"I've got to locate a crib for the baby." She ignored Albert, as she made a mental note to herself. On her to-do list, she'd forgotten to write down a bed for their youngest grandchild, fourteen-month-old Dean.

"Phooey. I remember when we used a dresser drawer for Matt, the time we visited my sister." Typically, Albert thought he had all the answers. As usual, Edna would have to do what needed to be done without explaining the details to him.

"We need a Christmas tree, but I can't put one up with you planted here in the middle of the room."

When he glared without saying a word, she knew his mind was working furiously on that problem.

"I've baking to do," she continued, hiding a smile of triumph and glancing up toward the ceiling. At once, she spotted a cobweb in the corner. She'd have to ask Beverly to run the broom around the edges of the ceiling and make certain to dust the chandeliers in the front hall and above the dining room table. Another mental note to add the request to her to-do list. *Crib, cobwebs.*

"I thought you and Mary were baking this afternoon. Isn't that why you went to the store this morning?"

Plainly, he had no notion of the time it took to bake the variety of breads, cookies and puddings required by Christmas tradition. He'd miss his plum pudding with hard sauce if that weren't on the menu.

"I've presents still to wrap and a few dozen cards to address."

"I can help with the cards."

This time, Edna couldn't help but laugh aloud. "The post office would never be able to decipher your physician's handwriting. The cards would either be marked as undeliverable or end up in some foreign country."

"Okay, okay. Enough already," Albert held up his hands in mock dismay, and his old familiar grin was back in place. "I'm sorry, sweetheart. I've been selfish. I'll sit quietly and read from now on."

Obviously, he'd already forgotten about the tree. Edna shook her head, not daring to speak for a minute. "It's not just that. I drive you to Providence once a week to have your knee x-rayed and see your doctor. Your next appointment is tomorrow morning and that means another day out of my schedule. If the storm hits and we get even half the snowfall they're predicting, we could get stuck in the city."

"What do you want me to do?" He knew her well enough by now to realize she had a plan.

"I'd like you to spend a few days with Diane."

Thirty-nine-year-old Diane was Edna and Albert's second child. She and her husband Roger lived with their fifteen-year-old son in Pawtucket, not far from the Blackstone Park Conservation District. Roger Junior, or "Buddy" as he was called, was an avid chess player and loved nothing better than to challenge his grandfather to a match. Whenever he visited his grandparents, Buddy carried his favorite chessboard with him and often persuaded Albert to play two games simultaneously.

Albert looked skeptical and opened his mouth to speak, but Edna hurried on. "If you stay with Diane, Roger and Buddy in Pawtucket, you'll be much closer to the clinic, and she can take you to your appointments. Besides the fact that she's a trained RN and works only part time, their downstairs study with its adjoining bathroom would make a perfect bedroom. You'd have privacy instead of sitting here in the middle of our living room. Best of all, Buddy's home from school this week. You two can play chess. It'll be good for your grandson to have you to himself. I know he'd love it, and you'll have your own personal aide."

She tried not to sound desperate in convincing Albert what fun it would be to spend time with the only one of their children who seemed to have been born with no sense of humor. Diane was kind and well-meaning, but tended to take life too seriously and to hover over her patients whenever she took occasional jobs in home health care. Ordinarily, it would drive Albert crazy to have someone always at his elbow, but in this case, it might be just the distraction he needed.

"I wanted to discuss this with you before calling Diane, but if you want a family Christmas this year, you must help me out. I need you to go where I won't have to worry about you and I won't have to spend my time taking care of your needs."

He thought for a moment before he agreed, somewhat reluctantly, that she should call their daughter.

Half an hour later, arrangements had been made for Diane, husband Roger and son Buddy to come for supper that evening and take Albert home with them. As Edna had known, Diane was delighted to be asked to help and, typical of this nurturing daughter, eager to tend to her father's every whim.

On the spur of the moment, Edna decided to phone Charlie Rogers and invite him to lunch the following day. She had met the police detective shortly after moving into the community when a friend's house had been robbed of valuable antiques. Edna had discovered the break-in and her friend lying half-conscious in the entryway of her home. Charlie had been the officer assigned to the case. Not long afterwards, Edna had been the prime suspect in the death of her handyman, another incident that put her in almost daily contact with Charlie. Through the challenge of proving her innocence, she and he had developed a mutual liking and respect. She was pleased when he showed a romantic interest in her youngest and only unmarried child.

Better yet, she knew he had a few days off, his chief at the police department having insisted on Charlie using some of his built-up vacation time. Why he hadn't gone skiing in Colorado with Starling was something between the two young people. Edna hoped it wasn't because the relationship was cooling off. However, since he had time on his hands and she needed all the help she could get, she felt no compunction in bribing him to hang Christmas lights around the yew trees at the front door and along the eaves of the house. She was certain she could also talk him into helping her find a tree for the living room, once Albert and his recliner were out of the way. Thinking of inside decorations, she decided to ask Charlie, Mary and the neighbors from across the street for an evening of drinks, hors d'oeurves and tree trimming. It would mean adding another party to an already busy week, but having friends help decorate would be much more fun than doing the job by herself.

Having done as much as she could for the moment, she prepared lunch, removed a chicken casserole from the freezer for supper, checked to see she had enough salad ingredients and started a rosemary cheese loaf in her bread machine. Her mood brightened as she prepared lunch and anticipated dinner with one of her children.

Unbidden, her thoughts turned to another family as Mary's words came back to her. "Kevin

Lockhorn has moved to town … Tom Greene's nephew."

Tom Greene. Tom. His face and smile and memories of the gentleness of the big man came flooding back. In a short time, they'd become good friends. Sharing a similar sense of humor had helped. And then too quickly, he was gone.

She thought of the portrait she'd sketched of him shortly after his death and wondered if his family would like to have it. She might dig it out and lay it aside, in case. She didn't know why she'd never offered it to Tom's daughter or grandson. *Perhaps*, Edna thought, *I haven't been quite ready to part with it.*

She shook her head to dispel sad memories and spent the next half hour sharing sandwiches and tea with Albert. By the time she headed next door, Benjamin was curled up on her husband's lap, and both man and cat were nodding off for a nap.

Edna passed by Mary's front door and proceeded to the back entrance where she noticed a bicycle leaning against the house. Since she was expected, Edna didn't knock but walked into the hallway which led to the kitchen. She'd just opened her mouth to call out "Hello" when she heard a voice raised in anger.

"She's ruining my life. I could *kill* her."

Chapter 3

As soon as Edna stepped into her neighbor's house, Hank came trotting in from the kitchen, tail wagging as he gave her a single welcoming bark. She was also greeted by a half-grown black cat who had been sleeping on a thick towel, folded atop the radiator that stood beneath the window next to the door. Ink Spot arched her back in a post-nap stretch and blinked curiously at Edna.

"Hello, Spot," Edna said, giving the cat's ears a scratch after first stroking Hank's head.

Eight months ago, when Starling first heard the moniker Mary had pinned on the dainty feline, Edna's daughter had been amused. "Leave it to you to give a dog's name to a cat," she'd said, cradling the newly-adopted kitten.

Mary had simply shrugged and grinned. "Spot doesn't mind. She likes her name. Better than Inky."

After that, nothing more was said about Spot's name being the least inappropriate.

Now, on this cold blustery day, the cheerful greetings from Mary's pets contrasted with the angry voice emanating from the other room. Apparently, Mary and her guest weren't yet aware of her arrival, so Edna pushed the outer door shut firmly enough to make noise and took time to hang her coat on a nearby wooden peg before striding into the kitchen. Hank followed close behind, but Spot stayed where she was, obviously reluctant to leave the warmth and comfort of her bed.

"Hi, Edna," Mary was leaning back against the counter at the opposite side of the room, holding a coffee mug in one hand and propping her elbow up with the other. "Come on in."

Apparently, Mary had heard Edna, but not the young woman whose voice had carried into the back hall. She spun around, her mouth half opened as she was caught in the middle of an obvious rant. She'd been so engrossed in what she was saying, she hadn't heard Edna's attempt to forewarn of her entrance. Mary's visitor was about Edna's height, five feet five, and nearly fifty years younger. Edna guessed the stranger to be about twenty years old.

"Meet Bethany Marco." Mary made the introduction and seemed relieved by the interruption. "She's just been fired from her day job."

Bethany, face mottled with unspent anger, was nonetheless able to look sheepish when she said, "Hello" in a much quieter voice than she'd used a minute ago. Her fiery blue eyes, olive-toned skin and long, dark hair made a lovely picture, despite her fury.

"Bethany, this is Edna Davies, my friend and neighbor."

The woman's discomfort turned to surprised delight at the introduction. "Oh, you're Benjy's owner. I've heard so much about you."

"Benjamin," Edna corrected automatically,

giving Mary a hard glare before smiling at Bethany. "I hope you've heard nice things." *And not about murders and mayhem,* she thought. Edna was never certain how much Mary told others about the dodgy escapades the two of them had experienced in the year and a half they had lived next door to each other.

"Of course. Mary says you're cool," Bethany assured her.

Picking up on what Mary had said about the young woman's plight, Edna looked at her with concern. "I'm sorry to hear you've lost your job. What is it you do?"

Bethany stared at Mary as if expecting her to explain, so with a shrug, their red-headed host said, "She works ... *worked* at CATS. That's how I know Bethany. We met when I started volunteerin' there."

Turning to Edna, Bethany interjected, "I'm a student at the university, so it wasn't a career job or anything. Minimum wage, but it pays for groceries and my share of the rent. Without it, I can't afford to live around here and still go to school. If I transfer to Boston and live with my parents, I'll lose too many credits which'll mean at least another semester before I graduate. That'll mean more expenses and more time before I get a job so I can start paying back my loans." She stamped her foot in frustration. "It's all a big mess and it's all Laurel's fault."

Edna thought for a minute, trying to remember why the name sounded familiar.

Correctly reading her puzzled expression, Mary said, "Laurel Taylor runs the cat shelter.

Remember? You met her this morning at Stop and Shop."

"Of course." Sensing that Bethany hadn't finished complaining about the injustice of it all, Edna asked, "What happened to make her fire you?"

"She says I was 'consorting with the enemy'," Bethany sputtered. "That is so totally not right." She smirked at Mary as if knowing the red-head would understand and agree.

Somewhat amused by what seemed an odd sort of incident for a cat shelter, Edna said, "Enemy?"

"Vincent Valmont," Bethany replied, as if this were all the answer necessary.

Edna frowned at Mary, waiting for clarification of the cryptic reply. At the same time, she flicked her eyes to the clock on the wall, hoping Mary would get the message that they had work to do and Edna couldn't spend all afternoon trying to decipher the problems of the young and emotional.

Interpreting the look, Mary pushed away from the counter and set down her mug. "Vinnie's a local kid," she said. "Been a prankster ever since I can remember. Been picked up by the police lots of times growing up, but he never did anything worth bookin' him for. Clownin' around, is all. He's nice enough now, far's I'm concerned." She smiled at her young visitor. "He's taken a shine to Bethany."

"He's a pest. He won't leave me alone." Cheeks reddening slightly in an attractive blush, Bethany turned to Edna. "He shows up. It's not my fault if he follows me around."

"I still don't understand what that has to do with

you being fired?" Edna moved to a nearby counter where she'd left her baking tins earlier that morning, but she remained half turned to indicate she was listening.

"Last summer, right after she bought the house and decided to turn it into a cat shelter, Laurel hired Vinnie to build some runs in her backyard. He did a great job," Bethany said, her face lighting up. "He's really good at building stuff." She seemed unaware of the sparkle in her eyes when talking about "the pest." As suddenly as the sun had come out, however, her face clouded over again. "When it was time for Laurel to give him his final payment, she short-changed him. That's what he says. She says she paid him in full and he's trying to cheat her."

"Why not simply produce her cancelled checks?" Edna asked.

Bethany shook her head. "It was a cash deal. Neither of them can prove how much Laurel paid him ... or didn't pay him." The young woman paused and looked down at the floor as if trying to decide what to say next. Several seconds went by before she looked up and spoke to Mary with a questioning frown. "Vinnie says Laurel was always flirting with him. Made him uncomfortable, her being so much older. He thinks she stiffed him because he rejected her. I don't like to spread rumors like that, but do you think it might be true?"

Mary thought briefly, then shrugged. "'S possible. Laurel plays up to all the men, but I don't think she means any harm. She goes to an assertiveness training class at the hospital. Maybe that's all it is and he misread the signals."

Bethany disagreed. "She kicked him out, told him never to come near CATS again. And she cheated him out of what she owed him. I wouldn't say that was so harmless. He can't even use her as a reference after all the work he did."

"It sounds like a case of his word against hers," Edna said, bringing Bethany's attention back to her. Again, Edna asked, "What does it have to do with you getting fired?"

"First off, I got the job through Vinnie. We're in a class together at the university. That's how we met. If our being friends wasn't reason enough, Laurel saw me with him this morning. Well, actually, I wasn't really *with* him." She sighed, as if explaining the details was becoming burdensome. "I stopped for coffee on my way to work and happened to run into him. He offered me a ride to Laurel's in his pickup. It was so cold this morning, I agreed. I practically froze walking from my place to the coffee shop and CATS was another mile away."

"And Laurel saw you together," Edna said, trying to speed up the story. Time was passing. She and Mary needed to get on with their baking. She was relieved to see Mary had already gotten out the flour, sugar and butter and was rummaging in the cupboard where she kept her bowls and cookie sheets. Edna walked to the refrigerator and took out a carton of eggs before returning to her place by the counter, as Bethany continued her rant.

"That's right. She saw me get out of his truck. And now she's saying I'm in cahoots with him. She said she can't trust me anymore, that I might do something to get even for him. She wouldn't let me explain, just told me to get out. And she shorted me a week's pay."

"Doesn't sound right, does it?" Mary said as she knelt on the floor in front of the cabinet. As she did so, Hank rose to come join her in examining the bowls. Laughing, Mary ordered him off to "hit the bricks" in the archway into the dining room before she ducked back to withdraw a baking sheet.

"You'd think she'd at least let you tell your side of things." Edna spoke to Bethany while she watched the dog's antics with amusement.

"She's too mean and vindictive and I'd like to …"

"My guess," Mary rose from the floor, interrupting Bethany, "is that she either doesn't have the money, or doesn't want to spend it. She's been recruitin' volunteers and I think she figures she doesn't need to pay someone if she can get the work done for nothing." At that thought, Mary gave Bethany a guilty look. "I'd stop going over there if it would get you your job back, but she'd just find some other volunteer to take my place."

Bethany wailed. "I know it's not your problem, but what am I going to do? Without that job, I won't be able to finish school next semester, and I've got only three classes left to graduate." The young woman's anger began to rise again, flushing her face anew. "I'm so mad, I could spit nails."

Mary handed a cookie sheet to Bethany. "Here. Wash your hands and start greasing these. Might as well work while you talk." As she began to measure flour into a bowl, she restated her opinion. "Do you suppose Laurel is using Vinnie as a convenient excuse to get rid of you, since you're the only paid worker she has left? I mean, even if you could convince her you're not scheming something with Vinnie, the real problem seems to be that she doesn't want to keep paying you."

"I bet you're right." Bethany shook her head in disgust. "It was the only job I could find to work around my class schedule, too. If I don't find something else, I'll have to tell my parents there won't be any graduation party next May, maybe ever. Nice Christmas present, huh?" She turned away, facing the dining room, but not before Edna saw tears brim in the young woman's eyes.

Mary must have noticed, too, because she broke the brief silence, providing a distraction as she explained to Edna, "Bethany's the first in her family to go to college. Her graduating means a lot to her parents."

"Is Laurel really that cruel and inconsiderate?" Edna asked as Bethany turned around, having wiped her tears away with a tissue from her pocket.

"Better believe it," Bethany said. "You know Doctor Jake and his wife?"

"Of course, he's Benjamin's veterinarian and she works with him at the clinic." Holding a bowl in the circle of one arm, Edna beat eggs with a metal whisk.

"Well, instead of going to the clinic, Laurel invites Roselyn over for tea whenever she--Laurel, that is--needs something. If Roselyn can take care of a sick cat or trim claws or bring over free medical samples, then cheapskate Laurel doesn't have to pay a vet bill."

"Roselyn doesn't have to go along with it," Mary pointed out, unwrapping a stick of butter.

"No, but she's so nice. She never refuses."

"I've heard that Roselyn is a soft touch when it comes to animals," Edna agreed.

Mary nodded, raised her eyebrows at Edna and spoke slowly, as if voicing a plan as it materialized in her mind. "Tomorrow's my volunteer morning at CATS. Since Laurel invited you to tea, why don't you come with me? Maybe we can appeal to her good side and work something out for Bethany."

Edna thought for a moment. She really shouldn't take the time, considering all she had to do, but then she studied the two other women. Mary's eyes twinkled, probably thinking what fun it would be to go on a spying caper. Bethany's face was aglow with hope. At that moment, Edna decided she didn't like the idea of a struggling student being cheated, particularly at the time of year when peace and good will should reign. Besides that, she knew how disappointed she and Albert would have been if one of their children had dropped out of college so close to graduation. Between Mary and herself, they might be able to persuade Laurel to take Bethany back for a few more months. Edna realized that, when it came to someone in trouble, she was as soft a touch as Roselyn, but Edna couldn't help herself. With a feeling of relief that she wouldn't have to explain herself to Albert, since he was going to be safely out of the way, she nodded her acquiescence. Still, she couldn't stop the thought that followed close behind -- *only five days until Christmas and I have so much to do.*

Chapter 4

Once Edna agreed to go with Mary to CATS the following morning, Bethany didn't stay much longer. As the young woman prepared to leave, Edna thought about how cold the day had been and remembered the bicycle resting against the side of the house.

"Did you ride your bike here from town?" she asked and wondered not only about the weather but also about how unsafe it was to cycle on the narrow, winding two-lane road that ran through their rural neighborhood.

"Only way I could get here," Bethany said, tugging a white knitted cap snugly over her dark hair and pulling gloves from a side pocket of her red ski jacket. "I can't afford a car, so I borrow whatever wheels I can. The bike belongs to Vinnie. He's trying to get his uncle to use it instead of the truck, but his uncle lets me borrow it." She grinned and Edna saw what might have been a conspiratorial gleam in the young woman's eyes as Bethany glanced up at the clock on the wall. "I better be going. I promised to have it back before Vinnie gets off work."

"Don't you get cold?" Edna shivered just thinking of bicycling on such a bitter, overcast day.

Bethany nodded vigorously. "You bet, but not as

cold as hitchin' or walkin'. Turning up her jacket collar, she added, "It's only a couple of miles. Could be worse."

"I don't like the thought of you hitchhiking," Mary piped up from where she had been spooning dough onto one of the greased cookie sheets. "This community might be one of the safest in the state, but you never know who might pick you up."

"I know, I know," Bethany said as she pushed the gloves tight between each finger. "And I thank you for your offer of taxi service, but I can't call you every time I want to go somewhere." She went over to Mary and gave her a one-arm, sideways hug. "You're a good friend, and I promise to be careful." She turned and strode toward the back hall, waving to Edna. "Nice to meetcha," she said as she left Edna and Mary to get on with their baking.

"What do you make of the allegations against Laurel Taylor?" Edna asked after she heard the outside door bang shut. "Could Bethany and her friend have misunderstood how much they were to be paid?"

"Hard to say," Mary said, rolling pieces of peanut butter dough into small balls before placing them on another of the cookie sheets. "Like you said, it's their word against hers, and they don't have any proof of how much they've already been paid."

"Makes it awkward for us to confront Laurel, especially if she's so callous that she would fire Bethany this close to Christmas." Edna sighed and stopped stirring her batter for the moment as she pondered the problem. "We need to be very careful not to upset Laurel if we're to help Bethany at all."

"That we will," Mary agreed and began to press the peanut butter balls with a fork.

"You know Laurel better than I do. What would you suggest?" Edna felt her irritation rise at Mary's seeming detachment. "How do we approach her?"

"Play it by ear. You'll think of something." Mary removed the first batch of cookies from the oven and slid in the next sheet. She had two ovens, which was one reason they were using her kitchen for their marathon baking project.

Not knowing whether to be irritated or complimented by Mary's deferring to her, Edna finally gave up trying to discuss their predicament. She returned to the task of making cranberry cake, and as she tucked Bethany's woes to the back of her mind, Mary brought up a new topic of concern.

"Heard from Starling?"

"She phoned yesterday." Edna poured her batter into a greased bread pan and looked around for a spatula.

"When're they flying in?" Mary asked, referring not only to Starling, but to Edna's third child and his family.

"I thought they were arriving the day after tomorrow, but she said Grant signed them up for a two-day cross-country trip out of Vail. It was a surprise Christmas present for her. Very thoughtful of him because he knows how much she enjoys her skiing trips to Colorado, but I'm afraid they've left Karissa to pack and get the two children ready. It also means they won't be flying home until Christmas Eve."

"They won't miss my party, will they?"

"Starling says they have an early flight that gets into Providence mid-afternoon, so they should arrive in plenty of time."

"Good. I'm looking forward to meeting your new daughter-in-law and the baby--besides seeing your granddaughter Jilly and Grant again, of course." Mary moved to the kitchen sink beside Edna to rinse out her bowl. "Shame they had to cancel their plans to visit last summer."

"I'm hoping the weather doesn't make them cancel Christmas plans, too," Edna said. "I wish they hadn't waited until the last minute to travel. If flights are delayed ..." She didn't finish the thought, determined not to let her worries ruin the holiday spirit for Mary, if not for herself. "How about finding a radio station with good Christmas music," she said, vigorously scraping the last of the batter from her bowl into the bread pan.

Thereafter, Edna made certain conversation remained on neutral, non-troublesome topics, and the two neighbors worked and chatted companionably. They even sang a few carols along with the all-music radio station Mary found. Hank decided to join in when they began "Away in a Manger" and their laughter halted not only their singing, but their work.

Since it was past five o'clock, Edna left Mary with a final pan of mint brownies in the oven and, taking a few ginger snaps and peanut butter cookies with her, she returned home to get ready for dinner with Diane and her family.

The chicken-divan casserole was heating in the

oven, and Edna had just finished making a Greek dressing for the salad when she heard a terrible choking and sputtering racket coming from the road. She knew she wouldn't be able to see outside past the glow of the porch light, but the din drew her to the window above the sink anyway. Peering out, she saw Roger's black Chevy Suburban rounding the driveway. She couldn't imagine her son-in-law's vehicle making such a dreadful noise. For one thing, Diane wouldn't stand for it. Sure enough, the horrific sound faded into the distance before Roger pulled to a stop.

"They're here," she called to Albert, hurrying to open the front door. Fifteen-year-old Buddy was the first to enter, giving his grandmother a quick kiss on her cheek before heading down the hall to find his grandfather.

"Hello, Mother," Diane also greeted Edna with a kiss. "Who is your neighbor in that junker of a pickup?" she asked, shedding her coat.

"Needs a muffler," commented Roger, bending to plant his kiss on Edna's cheek before following his wife to the coat closet.

"It *needs* to go to the old-car graveyard," Diane retorted, handing her husband a wire hanger.

Closing the door against the cold, Edna said, "I've never heard such a noise. I can assure you, it's no neighbor of ours."

"You don't have Christmas lights up," Diane said. She stood in front of the hall mirror and ran a brush through her shoulder-length blonde hair.

*You don't need to remind me,* Edna thought, feeling anew the pressure of preparing for the holiday without Albert's help.

"Granddad says it's time for a drink," Buddy announced, coming back into the hall. He was obviously unaware that he'd just saved his grandmother from saying something she might have regretted at that moment.

Perhaps it had been a look in her mother's eye, but Diane made no more mention of the lack of decorations or of the thunderous pickup as the family gathered in the living room for drinks and chatted amiably before a glowing fire. Soon, Albert and Buddy set up a chess board and began a match while Roger looked on. Diane and Edna went to the kitchen to get dinner on the table. The evening progressed pleasantly enough until Edna began clearing away the supper dishes. Setting plates in the kitchen sink, she looked out the window to see fat snowflakes falling slowly and silently. Roger's vehicle was already covered with a fine layer of white. She returned to the dining room with cookies and a pot of tea and urged her family to hurry through dessert.

Refusing Diane's offer to help with the dishes, Edna said, "This is probably the start of the big storm the weathermen have been predicting. I'll feel better if you leave soon and get home safely." She hoped her face didn't reflect her sinking feeling as she thought of cleaning up without her daughter's help which meant Edna would probably not get any greeting cards written that evening. Her to-do list wasn't getting any shorter as the time before Christmas drew nigh.

Soon, Buddy went upstairs to the bedroom to get

Albert's suitcase while Diane fetched her father's wool coat, hat and mittens. Roger went out to warm up the Suburban and brush away the snow.

"Are you sure you'll be okay here, sweetheart? I don't like leaving you with a storm coming on." Albert stuffed a paperback into an already stretched-out pocket in the green cardigan he wore over a yellow shirt.

"That's exactly why you need to leave, dear. If we're to get three feet of snow, as they're predicting, I might not be able to get you into the city for your doctor's appointment tomorrow." With mixed feelings of relief that he would be well tended and of sadness that she'd miss his company, Edna thought she might laugh and cry at the same time. Instead, she swallowed the lump in her throat and smiled. "I'll be fine. You'll be away for only a few days, and I'll be so busy getting the house ready, the time will fly. Besides, Charlie promised to be here tomorrow. If we get much snow, I'm sure he'll be willing to shovel me out. I'll be perfectly fine." She kissed him, wondering if she were trying to convince Albert or herself.

Donning her own winter coat, hat and gloves, Edna followed her family out to their car and waved them on their way. As the tail lights disappeared down the road, she closed her eyes and lifted her face to the sky, letting snowflakes land and melt on her nose and cheeks. She enjoyed the sight and feel of a winter snow. She hoped the storm wouldn't be as severe as the reporters feared, but she felt that snow enhanced the festive atmosphere this time of year.

"Hi, neighbor."

The voice of the young woman who lived across the street interrupted Edna's thoughts. She turned to greet Carol James whom she'd first known as Jaycee Watkins.

"I saw your company leave and hoped you'd have a few minutes to spare," Carol said. She looked like a marshmallow with stick legs in a thigh-length, white down coat. She wore no hat and her medium-brown hair was plaited into its usual single braid. Her hands were thrust deep into the coat's side pockets.

"Come in. I'll make some tea." Edna made her way back to the house and held the door for her visitor to precede her.

"Thanks, but I can't stay long. Gran has been filling me with so much tea, I think I might float away." Carol looked sheepish in the brighter light of the hall when she turned to face Edna. "Actually, I've come to ask a favor."

"O-kaaay," Edna said, drawing out the word as an image of her to-do list popped into her head. She hoped Jaycee's favor wouldn't be something time-consuming.

"I'm flying to Chicago in the morning." She paused, waiting for Edna to react to her news.

Edna frowned. "This is rather sudden, isn't it? So close to the holidays?"

"It *is* sudden," Carol agreed, "and a darned nuisance, but I guess the prosecutors want to go over my testimony once more. The trial starts right after New Year's."

The trial was the result of Carol, a

photojournalist, having caught arsonists in the act of burning down the house of a prominent banker. That accidental discovery was the reason she'd tried to hide under the alias of "Jaycee Watkins." She'd been shooting photos of holiday lights in one of Chicago's wealthier suburban neighborhoods just a year ago when she'd seen the fire and captured the criminals with her camera.

"They say it's really important," she went on, "or I wouldn't leave Gran alone right now." Her face brightened. "I'll be back in a couple of days, depending on how things go, but I'll definitely be back for Mary's party."

"I see," Edna smiled, remembering that Carol's boyfriend lived in the Chicago area. He would be joining Carol and her grandmother in Rhode Island for Christmas, but a couple of days in his city would be fun for the two young lovers. She didn't speak these thoughts aloud, but instead said, "And you would like me to check on Gran while you're away?"

It was a rhetorical question, but Carol answered anyway. "Yes, please. Just to make sure she's alright. I'll worry about her with the snow coming and all."

"Of course. I'll see that nothing happens to her," Edna said, biting back a laugh at her neighbor's transparent excitement. She had developed a fondness for Carol over the past several months and enjoyed the young woman's zest for life.

Edna also liked Carol's no-nonsense grandmother who had arrived from Florida before Thanksgiving and planned to stay through the New

Year. "Gran," as everyone called her, had grown up in Westerly, Rhode Island, a half-hour's drive south of Edna's neighborhood. Gran and her third husband moved to Florida when he retired. Widowed now, she had decided to spend a few months with her granddaughter and was looking forward to her first white Christmas in years. Edna figured she would simply have to make a daily phone call to the energetic and outspoken octogenarian--neither an unpleasant nor a time-consuming chore.

"You're a great neighbor, Edna." Carol gave her an impulsive hug. "I'd better get home and finish packing."

The snow was falling heavily when Edna opened the door to let Carol out. "I hope your flight won't be cancelled."

"Me, too. I don't want any further delays with this trial. I'm sick to death of it." Carol smiled optimistically as she waved goodbye and disappeared into the night.

Edna returned to the kitchen and had just finished washing dishes and tidying up the kitchen when Diane called to say they'd gotten home safely, the roads weren't too slippery yet, and Roger was settling Albert into the downstairs room.

Exhausted from the day's activities, Edna decided to go to bed and get an early start in the morning. Mentally reviewing her schedule for the next day, she realized with relief that Beverly Lewis, owner of Housekeeper Helpers, was coming in the morning with her assistant. At least the house will be spotless for the holidays, Edna thought. She was about to drift off to sleep when she remembered her promise to Mary's young friend. Thinking of how Albert was always admonishing her to "just say no," she wondered why she had agreed to accompany Mary to the cat shelter. *Bethany's trouble with Laurel Taylor is none of my business.* Her thoughts segued into planning what she needed to accomplish the next day. *Charlie's coming for lunch. What can I serve him that's quick? How much snow are we going to get tonight? Will the weather delay my children arriving in time for Christmas? Where will I find a nice tree at this late date? Four days to Christmas. Only four days left until Christmas.*

With the image of a calendar and her to-do list spinning around in her head, it was another hour before she fell into a fitful sleep.

Chapter 5

The next morning, Edna was up before dawn. She jumped out of bed and hurried to the window, pleasantly surprised and greatly relieved to see the amount of snow that had fallen barely covered the grass. What she could see of the road was clear except for a narrow strip along the far edge.

She surprised herself by being half disappointed that the storm hadn't dropped an inch or two more, enough to give the landscape a Christmas-card appearance. The other half of her was happy the storm hadn't been severe enough to impair travel, so humming a few bars of "Let it Snow, Let it Snow, Let it Snow," she showered, dressed and went downstairs to greet Benjamin. After starting the coffee, she took a blueberry muffin from the freezer to thaw and was about to scramble an egg when the telephone rang.

"Mornin', Miz Davies," came a nasal greeting down the line.

"Beverly?" Edna wasn't certain, but it sounded like her cleaning woman.

"'S me alright. I got the flu, Miz Davies. I know this is a real bad time, but I won't be able to clean your house today."

Edna hoped her distress didn't reflect in her voice when she said, "I can help Junie. We'll manage. The important thing is for you to rest and get well."

Junie Williams was Beverly's employee. Housekeeper Helpers consisted of only the two women, although many people wondered why Beverly didn't expand, since she had a page-long waiting list. When questioned, she always replied, "You want somethin' done right, you gotta do it yerself."

"Junie won't be comin' along neither. She's sicker than me."

Edna felt panic bubbling up from her stomach into her throat, but before she could think of a sympathetic reply the doorbell rang. Distracted, she gave Beverly assurance that Edna didn't feel, wished the housekeeper a speedy recovery and rang off. Trying to think of what cleaning tasks would absolutely have to be done and what could be swept under the rugs, so to speak, she headed for the front door, muttering, "Who … at this hour?" It was not yet seven o'clock.

"Hi, Edna. I smelled coffee." Charlie Rogers grinned from inside a fleece hat that Edna knew was called a "mad bomber." Silly looking, she'd always thought, but good protection against the crisp morning coldness.

In her current crisis, she began to ponder what jobs Charlie might be willing to do. No, she silently chided and joked, she wouldn't ask him to mop the floors. Unable to keep from smiling at the thought, however, she stepped aside and let him in. She felt cheered at the sight of him and, even in her distress, couldn't help but laugh. "You're here early. It isn't quite time for lunch."

His cheeks turned a shade redder, and she suspected it wasn't all due to the outside temperature. "I was in the neighborhood. I hope I'm not disturbing you, but I did see your lights on."

The thought flicked through her mind that he might be missing Starling, but she wouldn't ask. Whatever was going on between her daughter and the detective was none of her business--unless, of course, he were to bring up the subject himself. Aloud, she said, "It's too soon for lunch, but you're just in time for breakfast. How about sharing some blueberry muffins and scrambled eggs?"

"Be still my heart," he quipped, removing his hat, gloves and down parka. "I swear, Edna, if you weren't married …"

"Stop your nonsense." She slapped his arm gently and pretended to scowl before breaking into another laugh. "Come in and grab a cup. Tell me why you're lurking around my house at this hour, other than your love of my cooking."

Without immediately answering, he stepped farther into the hall, laid his outer gear on a nearby chair and turned back to her. "Have you seen anyone riding a bicycle along the road recently?"

She nodded. "As a matter of fact, Mary's young friend Bethany rode a bike out here from town yesterday afternoon." She shook her head, shutting the door. "Can you imagine? In *this* weather?"

"No, this would have been after the storm, late last night or early this morning. I saw tracks in the snow at the side of the road about a half mile back, and I'm wondering how far into your neighborhood they'd come."

All thoughts of her housecleaning problems forgotten for the moment, she frowned. "I don't think Bethany would have bicycled back here in the dark, but we can ask Mary. She'll be over later."

At that moment, Benjamin appeared in the hallway to greet a familiar friend. Charlie bent to pick him up, stroking the cat's ginger fur as he followed Edna into the kitchen. Depositing the cat on a cushioned chair, the police detective strode to the coffee pot to pour himself a cup while Edna took a few more muffins from the freezer to heat in the microwave.

"Is that what brings you here so early?" she asked as she cracked an egg into a stainless steel bowl. "Are you looking for people who bicycle in storms? Don't tell me you're on a case when you're supposed to be on vacation."

Holding his steaming mug of coffee in both hands, he leaned back against the kitchen sink to watch as she prepared breakfast. "When you told me that Albert was staying with Diane and her family for a few days, I thought you might need help with more than just hanging a few Christmas lights. I'm at your disposal for the entire day." Spreading his arms wide, he gave her a courtly bow, careful not to spill his drink.

Edna chuckled as she placed a skillet onto a lighted gas burner. "That's very thoughtful of you, and I can certainly use your help, but tell me why you asked about bicycles. You've roused my curiosity."

"Those tracks I saw might be connected to a

strange situation going on in town," he said. "Someone's borrowing bicycles."

"*Borrowing* bikes? Not *stealing* them?" She hastened to defend Mary's friend. "Bethany borrowed a bike, but she said she had permission."

"I don't think this would be Mary's friend. It's kinda weird." He sighed and lifted his coffee mug toward his lips, but lowered it again before taking a sip. Staring into the brown liquid, he spoke haltingly as if thinking aloud. "The snow had probably stopped or the tracks would have been covered, at least partially." He raised his eyes to meet hers. "Do you know when the storm ended last night?"

"No idea. I went to bed early." She whisked the eggs and poured them into the hot frying pan. Picking up a spatula, she began to stir the mixture as it cooked.

"I'll check with the guys on duty, but I'm thinking it might have been around eleven. Sometime before midnight, I'm pretty sure."

"Who would be riding around here at that hour?" she asked, briefly glancing up from the eggs. "It's so cold and this road doesn't have many street lights."

"I don't know if my bike thief would ride out this far." He paused, then spoke as if an idea had just occurred to him. "Maybe those tracks have nothing to do with the bike-napper I'm looking for. Maybe it was just some teenager who made the tracks along the road. Maybe visiting friends. Kids are impervious to cold. You should know that." He smiled at the mother of four and grandmother of seven.

"Silly of me not to remember," she said, rolling her eyes. She scooped eggs onto two plates which she then handed to him. "Go sit and eat while it's hot. I'll bring the muffins, and I want to hear more about your case. I'm intrigued."

They ate in silence for several minutes before Charlie spoke again. "The first report we got on this bicycle mystery was three nights ago. A local fellow rode his bike to the pool hall 'cause he knew he'd be having a drink or three. Left the bike outside, as he's done before. When he came out around one in the morning, the bike was gone. Bartender called us. On his way to the site, our rookie spotted a bike about a block from the bar, so he took the guy over to look. Sure enough, it was his, so naturally we thought he'd forgotten where he'd left the thing. He'd had a few beers by the time he left the hall."

"Smart of him to ride his bike instead of driving," Edna remarked.

"Yes, well, same thing happened again night 'fore last. This time the bike belonged to a student. Same M.O. Kid played pool until sometime after midnight but swore he hadn't had more than three beers the whole time. When he left the place, he couldn't find his bike. This time, it was found across the street and down a couple of storefronts."

"Very peculiar," Edna murmured, sipping her coffee. "Did you stake out the place?"

Charlie gave a laugh. "You're ahead of me, Edna. Not exactly a stake-out, but the night patrol is making a point of cruising up and down that street regularly. Only thing is, nobody rode a bike to the bar last night, what with the snow and all. That's why I was surprised to see those tracks this morning. I talked to our dispatcher and the only bike the patrol spotted was behind the new restaurant in town."

"Krispin's Kitchen?" Edna mentioned the name she'd recently heard from her neighbors, Carol and Gran.

"That's the one."

"Gran's been baking rolls for them and making soup, too, from what Carol tells me."

Charlie raised an eyebrow which Edna correctly interpreted as curiosity.

"Apparently, the owner is an old friend of Gran's. The daughter manages the place and will inherit it someday. Gran likes to keep busy and loves to cook, so it works out for her and for the diner."

"Hmmm," he murmured. "I've been wantin' to check out the place. Now I will for sure. Gran's cooking is nearly as good as yours."

Edna laughed. "You flatterer. I know Gran is a better cook than I. You can say so without hurting my feelings."

He laughed, too. "Can't say for sure. I'll have to keep taste testing, I think."

Smiling briefly to acknowledge the compliment, Edna returned their conversation to the mystery. "Did you discover whose bike it was, the one left at the dumpster?"

"Patrol spoke to the restaurant manager--guess that would be Gran's friend's daughter. She said it belonged to one of her workers, so that one has turned out to be a false alarm." Charlie ran a hand through his curly hair and shook his head. "This morning, we have mysterious tracks in the snow, but no stolen bike. Doesn't make much sense, does it?"

The question was rhetorical, so Edna ignored it and asked one of her own. "Has nobody spotted the culprit, either riding off or returning?"

"Not as far as we know." He picked up his coffee mug, drained it and leaned forward as he placed it back on the table. "That's why I was hoping maybe you'd seen someone. The snow's already melted on the road, except in some shady places. That's where the tracks are still visible. The last ones I saw were about a quarter mile back towards town."

Edna shook her head. "Other than Mary's young friend pedaling out here yesterday afternoon, I don't know of anyone who bikes at this time of year. I find it hard to imagine someone biking home, only to turn around and go back to leave their bike in town--and certainly not in the dark of night." She grinned with amusement. "But then, we've lived here less than two years, so I'm not familiar with all the quirks of my neighbors."

Charlie chuckled. "People have been known to do stranger things than that." He grew serious when he added, "You're right, of course. Doesn't seem sensible, but I've gotta ask the questions and cover all bases.

Shaking her head over what seemed like bizarre behavior, Edna reached for Charlie's empty plate, stacked it onto hers and took them to the sink. She raised the coffee pot in a "want a refill" gesture. When he nodded, she filled his mug and topped off hers. Once she'd sat down again, she said, "Why would someone come all the way out here on a bicycle? We're, what … about two miles from town?"

"It would be a good way to scout out a place," Charlie said, joining in the speculation exercise. "Quiet, slow, methodical. If he's spotted, he'd probably be considered more of a nutcase than anything else." His gaze sharpened, as if realization had dawned.

With a short intake of breath, Edna also understood the implications. "Do you think it could be someone after Carol again?"

He nodded slowly, frowning. "That thought just occurred to me. Like you said, why would someone pedal this far out of town only to go back again-- and in the dark?"

"Why do you suppose the bikes aren't returned to the same spot? If they were, their disappearance might not be noticed. It's almost as if he's daring you to catch him, don't you think?"

Charlie shook his head. "Could be he's being cautious in case the owner comes out as the guy's putting the bike back. Or, the bike's owner might be out looking, and maybe his buddies, too. More of a chance for the thief to get caught if he goes back to the exact spot. Might be also, he's dropping the bike close to where he's parked a car. Quicker getaway and, again, less chance of being caught."

Edna thought for a moment. "I hope you're wrong about someone casing this neighborhood,

Charlie, but we can't take a chance. Carol left for Chicago this morning, and Gran's home alone."

"Do you think Gran might have seen someone? I don't want to scare her, but I'll need to ask."

"Could you have your patrol guys keep an eye on the house, so you don't have to worry her unnecessarily?"

He frowned, shaking his head. "I'll have to talk to her, if only to make sure she keeps her doors locked, but maybe I won't have to mention our concern that someone might be targeting her house. After all, we're only speculating at this point. I'll ask the shift supervisor about an extra patrol in the area, but we're short-handed right now, what with holiday leave on top of the flu going around."

Edna considered his words for a minute before nodding. "You're right. We can't keep this from her entirely. From what Carol has told me, her grandmother sometimes putters in that kitchen until midnight or later and then goes upstairs to read in bed for another hour or so. She might have seen or heard something. We'll have to wait a bit before we go over there, though. Because she stays up so late, she sleeps in. I don't think we should bother her until lunchtime, at the earliest."

As she spoke, Edna looked up at the wall clock. "Oh dear, I didn't realize it was so late. Mary will be here any minute. We're going over to CATS. You know as well as I that if anyone has been riding a bicycle along this road, Miss Nosy-Parker will have seen him … or her." Edna smiled at the thought of her curious and eccentric neighbor as she scooped up the coffee cups and muffin basket from the kitchen table and put them on the counter. Turning to Charlie, she motioned him toward the front hall. "Before she gets here, let me show you where the outside Christmas lights are and what I have in mind for decorating the yew trees."

They were standing at the edge of the driveway, studying the eaves, when Mary pulled up in her green ragtop Jeep.

"Whatcha doin'?" she asked, jumping out and striding over to stand beside them. She looked up at the roof to see what might be of interest.

"Hi-ya, Mary," Charlie greeted. "We're just checking to see if the chimney's big enough for Santa's visit."

She laughed and punched him playfully on the arm. "Go on."

Edna, reminded of time passing before the jolly man's journey, interrupted the bantering. "Lights on the yew trees will be enough decoration for the outside, but if you have time, a string along the eaves would be nice. I'll hang a wreath on the door, but I haven't bought it yet."

Charlie said, "I'm proposing a sleigh and a few reindeer on the roof. What do you think, Mary?"

"That's too involved," Edna said, uncertain as to whether Charlie was teasing or not. "Keep it simple. We still have to get a tree and decorate inside the house."

Mary, looking from one to the other, opened her mouth to speak, but Edna went on quickly, saying to Charlie, "Why don't you tell Mary about your mysterious bicyclist while I run in and get my pocketbook."

"Nope." Mary was shaking her head at Charlie when Edna returned. "I'll keep my eye out, though. You ready, Edna?"

Surprised but relieved that Mary didn't seem inclined to hang around talking "cops and robbers" with the detective, Edna turned to him. "Do you need anything else from me before I go? We shouldn't be more than an hour." She raised questioning eyebrows at Mary to confirm her statement.

"That's right. I don't spend more than that at CATS or Laurel would have me cleanin' her house and buyin' the groceries."

Edna's final words to Charlie as she climbed into the Jeep were a reminder. "Keep it simple, please." As they pulled away from the house, she spotted him in the side-view mirror. Grinning broadly, he was pulling a cell phone from his pocket.

Chapter 6

Once they were on their way, Edna tried to force the idea of someone spying on the neighborhood to the back of her mind. On a bicycle, no less. Absurd. She almost laughed aloud thinking of a hit man pedaling away from a crime scene, but less than a year ago, she had come face-to-face with the last villain to show up in the area and knew it was no laughing matter. Concentrating her attention on the upcoming visit to CATS, she wondered again why she had volunteered to accompany Mary on such a seemingly hopeless mission.

*Albert's always accusing me of being a soft touch. Perhaps he's right and I have to learn to say "No" more often. Too late this time.*

Aloud she said, "Tell me more about Laurel. If we're to persuade her to give Bethany her job back, I would like to know as much about the woman as possible. You've already told me what a flirt she is--something I saw for myself yesterday morning," she added, remembering the woman clinging onto Jake's arm. "Do you suppose she learns that sort of behavior in the assertiveness training class?"

Mary shook her head. "Not the classes I've been to. Probably her own interpretation, if you ask me."

Edna tucked another piece of information about her neighbor to the back of her mind, promising herself she'd ask Mary about her assertiveness class experience one day. For the moment, she wanted to know about the person they were on their way to visit. "I get the impression that she pinches her pennies, makes a dreadful pot of tea, and hasn't been in the business of rescuing cats for very long. Since this past summer?"

"That's right." Mary glanced briefly at Edna before returning her eyes to the road. There were few cars out that morning, but she was a careful driver who also paid constant attention to the side and rear-view mirrors. "Here's what I know," she began and then launched into what, for Mary, was a long speech.

"Laurel bought the house last summer when she moved here from somewhere in the Midwest. The day she moved in, she found three cats hiding in the basement. Previous owners were gone by then, but they'd left food and water, so Laurel knew the cats had been left intentionally. Right after that, she discovered a stray living under the back porch."

"Had she run an animal shelter before moving to this area?" Edna was curious as to how someone chose an occupation.

Mary shook her head. "She told me with all the cats around, the idea popped into her head. Said she found out it didn't cost much to start up, so she thought it might be a way to pay her monthly bills. I get the feeling she has money and is careful how she spends it.

"She got to know Jake and Roselyn when she took the cats to their clinic to be checked over. Since Laurel was new to town and getting established, Jake didn't charge her for his initial services. I think she's been taking advantage of his generosity ever since, and that might also be another reason why she decided to turn her house into a shelter. She takes in strays or cats whose owners can't or won't keep them any longer. Strays she gets for free, of course, but she charges people who want to find another home for a family pet. Small amount, but she does get something."

"I suppose that's reasonable," Edna said. "She must have to pay for food and veterinary care."

"She might have an occasional charge for Jake's time or for a prescription, but Roselyn stops in at CATS whenever she has some spare time from the clinic, usually once or twice a week. If there're any newcomers, she checks them over first to see if they might need Jake's expertise. She doesn't charge Laurel anything and sometimes even brings her free medical samples. Laurel's adoption fees are really low, but I found out that she pads the cost with veterinary expenses, even if the cat didn't need any special care. Seems people will object to paying almost any adoption fee, but won't blink an eye over a vet item."

"Sounds like she's got quite a little business going. It *is* nice that the cats eventually find homes, though. I guess she needs to make money somehow and if Roselyn doesn't mind ..." She was about to say more, but at that moment, Mary slammed on the brakes, pitching Edna forward.

They had reached an intersection in the middle of town, and although the traffic light was green, Mary came to a dead stop. "You okay?" She turned to Edna, shouting to be heard above the growing racket.

Edna had thrown up her hands, grabbing hold of the dashboard in an instinctive reaction, but the seat belt had saved her from any harm. Only a little shaken, she nodded to reassure Mary and looked up to see an old, battered pickup truck lurching and sputtering its way across their path. Smoke billowed from the tail pipe as the vehicle crawled through the intersection, a gray-haired, grizzled old man bent over the steering wheel, eyes intense and fixed straight ahead. Edna remembered the noise she'd heard the evening before about the time Diane and her family arrived for supper.

She looked up at the green traffic light and then over at Mary, raising her eyebrows in silent question, since she probably couldn't have been heard above the noise. Fortunately, there were no other cars in sight.

Mary wasn't looking at Edna. She was grinning as she watched the ancient truck cross in front of them and disappear down the side street. When the noise had abated enough so she could be heard, she said, "Codfish" and remained at the light that was now red in their direction.

"Codfish?" Edna queried. A memory came back to her as soon as the word was out of her mouth. "You mean that was Codfish McKale? Aleda Sharp's hit-and-run victim from last year?"

"Yep. I'm sorry she felt her family had to leave town, and in such a hurry, but I'm sure glad Gran and Carol bought the house. They're nice." The traffic light turned green and Mary drove forward.

"Speaking of Carol, she stopped by last night." And for the remainder of the trip through town and into older residential sections, Edna filled Mary in on their neighbor's trip to Chicago. She finished with her idea to have Gran, Mary and Charlie over for munchies, mulled wine and tree trimming as soon as Charlie could help her pick up a tree. "I'll be happy to feed everyone in exchange for help in getting my house decorated. That's one of the more time-consuming tasks on my to-do list."

"Sure, I'll be glad to help. Sounds like fun. Can Hank and Spot come, too?"

"Of course. Benjamin will have a few treats to share with them, I suspect."

Mary chuckled. "They'll like that." She glanced at Edna. "Hey … why don't we go get your tree when we finish at Laurel's, before we head back home?"

Edna didn't have a chance to answer. Mary again hit the brakes, forcing her passenger against the seat belt once more.

"I wish you'd quit doing that," Edna complained, but Mary wasn't listening.

"Wonder who that is?" Apparently distracted by their conversation, she had swerved into the driveway that ran beside a gingerbread-adorned house without looking and had nearly rear-ended a car already parked there. The driver had left little room for another vehicle. "Could've pulled up farther," Mary muttered, backing into the street and parking along the roadside shoulder.

The driveway at the side of the house led to a single-car garage at the back of the property, so there was room for several cars to park bumper-to-bumper. The bright blue compact currently in the drive wasn't very big. Mary was right, the owner could have left room for another vehicle. Apropos to nothing, Edna noticed that the last two digits of the license plate were thirty-two, her younger son's age.

"Maybe the person isn't staying long and didn't want to get blocked in," she suggested, trying to smooth Mary's ruffled feathers.

The two women left the Jeep, crossed a narrow strip of lawn and trudged up the railed steps to a wide, wooden porch. Edna, ahead of Mary, was about to ring the bell when the front door burst open and a woman staggered out backwards.

"You'll be sorry. You'll see," she said. Her voice wasn't loud, and the words came out like the hiss of a coiled snake. Spinning around, she bumped into Edna, causing her to stumble back into Mary.

The woman, dressed in a long, black wool coat and knit cap, clutched a black handbag in gloved fingers. She backed up a step in surprise, pausing for only a second before brushing wordlessly past the two women. Clearly upset, she raced toward the blue car, started the engine and reversed into the street. It was only then that she stopped to glare for several heartbeats before throwing the transmission into gear and speeding off, tires screeching. Edna and Mary, left on the porch, could only stare, stunned and gaping.

"Wow. What was that all about?" Mary's question brought Edna out of her stupor.

"Nothing to worry over," Laurel stood in the

doorway and answered with a shrug as she looked after the quickly disappearing vehicle. Her smug expression turned to a smile of greeting as she turned to her new visitors. "How nice to see you again," she said to Edna before nodding at Mary, as if nothing unusual had happened. "You're just in time to help me put up some last-minute decorations. Jake will be here soon to take some Santa pictures and I want everything in place." She whirled on her heel and hurried back into the house, obviously expecting them to follow. "I'll put the kettle on. The tea can steep while we work."

She disappeared down a narrow hall while Edna and Mary stopped to hang their coats on a free-standing rack in the corner behind the front door. The house seemed lopsided to Edna. All the rooms were on the left as she stood looking down the hall into the kitchen. The wall to her right had only one window. It overlooked the driveway and was nearly hidden by the coats on the rack. A straight-backed wooden chair rested against the wall, convenient for sitting to remove or don boots. Narrow stairs, running parallel to the hall, led to rooms above. To her immediate left was a closed door.

Interrupting Edna's examination of the surroundings, Mary moved to open the door and entered a good-sized living room.

"Hey, Edna. Look at this," she called just as Laurel reappeared from the back of the house.

"The tea's brewing. We'll have a cup when we're through," she said and motioned for Edna to precede her into the room where Mary was now gazing in wonder.

A six-foot tree, standing in front of a broad window, was covered with cat decorations of all descriptions. Edna spotted a red Christmas ball in the shape of a cat's head. She laughed delightedly at a miniature porcelain cat sitting inside a teacup hanging by its handle. She was amazed and enchanted with the number and variety of feline themes displayed among the branches. The usual string of multi-colored lights was wound around the tree, as well as a homemade string of popcorn.

She might have studied the tree for several more minutes had it not been for something rubbing against her leg. She looked down to see a small white cat dusting the bottom of Edna's black wool slacks with its fur. Chuckling, she bent to scratch its ears. "Do you smell Benjamin on me, pretty one," she cooed.

"She can't hear you. That one's deaf," Laurel said. She'd crossed to a card table set up at the back of the room and stacked with several boxes of Christmas ornaments. Wide strips of red ribbon with greeting cards attached hung off one side of the table. She picked up a box of silver and gold glass balls before coming back to stand beside Edna next to the tree. "Pure white cats with blue eyes are always deaf. Did you know that?"

"No, I didn't." Edna bent to pick up the cat, since it appeared to be affectionate and not at all leery of her. "Why is that?"

The woman shrugged. "It has something to do with the gene that gives the eyes their blue color. I looked it up on Wikipedia--you know, the computer site that has answers to everything. They say a cat with one blue and one brown eye will be deaf only on the side with the blue eye. Isn't that weird?" Before Edna could reply, Laurel nodded toward the cat. "She's not up for adoption. She gets scared if she thinks she's alone, prowls the house yowling for company. I have two other cats who seem to know what she needs, and they take pretty good care of her."

Edna was thinking how much nicer Laurel seemed when she was talking about her animals and not acting like a teenaged flirt. Before she could dwell on how complex the woman seemed, Mary spoke up.

"Black cats are the hardest to adopt out. Isn't that right?" She walked over to the other two ladies, holding a sleek, short-haired black cat in her arms. She leaned toward Edna so the white and black felines could touch noses.

"The white one's name is Snowflake and the black one's Charcoal. Auntie Bea is upstairs. I've put her in the room with a little calico kitten I got recently. Auntie Bea's my old female and mothers the rest of them, especially the new ones. Something about her seems to make other cats accept her immediately. I'm fortunate to have her. Makes introducing new cats into the house a whole lot easier than it would be ordinarily."

"Why are blacks hard to place?" Edna was curious about Mary's comment.

"Superstitious nonsense," Mary said with a scowl. "Unfortunately, it's the cats who suffer."

Laurel reached out to stroke Charcoal. "Some shelters won't allow anyone to adopt a black for the entire month of October. It's tragic, but some people are abusive at Halloween."

"I suppose it's because black cats have been associated with witchcraft for centuries," Edna said, giving Snowflake a final gentle hug before putting her down.

"That's right," Mary scoffed, shaking her head. "Witches' familiars. Even in this supposedly enlightened age." She put a now-wiggling Charcoal down beside his friend and the two felines scampered out of the room.

"We have work to do, ladies" Laurel said abruptly. "Hang these Christmas balls along the garland on the banister in the hall, if you would, Edna. On the outside, please. Otherwise, the cats will have them all battered off within the hour." She smiled as she thrust the box into Edna's hands.

Returning to the card table, she picked up a clump of mistletoe with a slender red ribbon wrapped around the stem, its ends curled through the green leaves of the plant. "I need you to hang this from the light fixture in the front hall, Mary." She reached for a smaller sprig with a few berries on it. "This one I carry with me." Holding it over her head so the other women would catch her meaning, Laurel rolled her eyes and grinned. "I'm going to hang the ribbons with the Christmas cards along the hallway. Don't you think that'll look nice?"

Standing on the stairs and bending over the banister to attach Christmas balls to the garland, Edna wondered how she'd gotten roped into decorating someone else's house when she still had her own to do. Hindering her progress were the black cat and his white friend who chased each other around her feet and batted at the shiny balls as she took them out of the box. It was a distraction she enjoyed, though, and she teased the half-grown felines with a string of tinsel she'd found caught on one of the hooks.

When the last of the glass balls had been hung, Edna remembered that she and Mary needed to broach the subject of Bethany's job, or at least ask about the back pay. She looked over to where Mary was standing on the hall chair, tying mistletoe to the base of the ceiling's light fixture. As Laurel pinned ribbons along the wall in the hallway leading to the kitchen, she carried on a stream of conversation, mostly about the customers who had sent the cards. Realizing she needn't reply to any of the woman's comments, Edna sat on the stairs, absently playing with the kittens as she thought about how to open a delicate subject in which she had no business. She had nearly decided on a plan of action when she heard Laurel squeal.

"Quick, Mary. Jake just pulled up in his van. I want the mistletoe secure before he gets to the door."

Glancing out the side window behind the coat rack, Edna could see that a white van was indeed parked in the driveway. Jake was sliding out of the driver's side. Laurel, halfway down the hall, must have super sensitive ears, Edna thought. As she continued to watch the scene outside, someone in a Santa Claus suit climbed down from the passenger side. From that angle, Edna could only see his head and shoulders, topped by a red stocking cap and wrapped in a furry collar. The figure disappeared toward the rear of the van without turning her way.

Flapping her hands in agitation, Laurel urged Mary to restore the chair to its place against the wall and instructed Edna to leave the empty ornament box on the table in the living room. While they obeyed, Laurel plucked their coats from the rack, handed one to Mary and held the other out to Edna as she returned to the hall.

"Thanks so much for your help. I know you both must have a ton of things to do, and I'm going to be awfully busy with this photo shoot. I'm so sorry about tea, but maybe another time." These last words were directed at Edna as Laurel practically pushed them out onto the porch.

Meeting Jake on the porch steps, Edna and Mary stopped for a few seconds to greet the veterinarian before crossing the lawn to the Jeep. Santa was leaning in the van's open side door, rummaging through boxes. All Edna could see was a broad, red backside trimmed in fluffy white. Whoever was in the suit finally stood, turned and glowered at them as Mary maneuvered a U-turn in the road to head back toward town.

"I hope that man puts on a happier face for the pictures," Edna said.

Santa's beady eyes looked familiar, but with fake white eyebrows, mustache and beard, she couldn't think of whom she was reminded. She twisted to look out the back window at the costumed figure, trying to place him. Behind the less-than-jolly elf, her eye caught another movement and she watched as Laurel pulled Jake into the hall where Mary had hung the mistletoe.

Chapter 7


While they had been inside CATS, the cloud cover had lifted, which raised Edna's spirits as well, so it wasn't with a great deal of regret that she said, "We never had a chance to talk to Laurel about Bethany's job,"

"We sure got the bum's rush, didn't we," Mary said, sliding her eyes toward Edna before refocusing on the road.

Edna chuckled. "More of her assertiveness training, I suppose."

Traffic had picked up during the hour they'd spent at CATS, so Mary was keeping her eyes on the road. "Wanna go get a Christmas tree?"

"Yes, that's a good idea. Laurel's looked so pretty, I'm in the mood. Let's go to Schartner Farms over in Exeter, shall we?" Edna felt like going to a place that was guaranteed to be filled with Christmas cheer. She certainly had a lot to do at home, but every item crossed off her list was another step forward. "Working on Laurel's stairwell made me think about my own banister. Schartner's has those evergreen ropes and a big selection of decorative wreaths. I can also pick up a couple of my favorite traditional poinsettias."

Eventually, Edna found everything she was looking for, plus a few additional gift items she couldn't resist. By the time they reached home, they had been gone a little more than four hours. Edna gasped as Mary pulled into the driveway, wondering for a second or two if they'd arrived at the wrong house. The first thing that caught her eye was a large, white wireframe sleigh complete with two full-sized reindeer in the middle of the circular drive. The cow--Edna assumed the slightly smaller figure with no antlers would be the female--had her head bent as if grazing. The twelve-point buck stood protectively by his mate with head raised and turned to look sideways toward the road as if he'd been startled by the car that had just pulled in.

As the Jeep passed this central display, Edna's gaze was caught by a larger-than-life Santa Claus, waving to them from the rooftop beside the chimney. When Mary pulled up to stop behind a white pickup truck, Edna dropped her eyes to the row of translucent plastic icicles dripping from the eaves and the strings of multi-colored lights twinkling around the yew trees.

*Oh my goodness*, she thought. *I wonder what Albert will make of this. Good thing he isn't home. In his weakened condition, his heart might not take it,* she mentally joked.

Albert had been the one to decorate the outside of the house--or supervise the boys when Matthew and Grant were old enough to help their father. He had always kept outside decorations simple, typically a single string of lights along the edge of the roof. To complete the exterior holiday presentation, Edna would set a single, battery-powered candle in each of the downstairs front windows.

As the women got out of the car, mouths agape at the sight of the house and yard, Charlie appeared on the brick path from the south side of the house. Behind him walked a man Edna had never seen before. The stranger was carrying a metal ladder and a red toolbox that he stopped to put in the back of the pickup before joining them. As he dropped the equipment into the bed of the truck, Edna noticed the logo emblazoned across the driver's door, "Honeydew Home Repairs."

"What do you think?" Charlie asked as he approached, smiling broadly and stretching his arms wide.

Edna, still stunned, circled slowly, trying to take it all in. As she looked from sleigh to twinkling trees to the man on the roof, she began to imagine her grandchildren arriving at the house and catching sight of the scene. At the thought, she burst into a laugh of pure delight. "It's marvelous, Charlie. How did you get all this done in so short a time? And where did it all come from?" She stared anew at the sleigh and reindeer. Sculpted of wire with white lights outlining their shapes, they would look magnificent on a dark night.

"You brought these from your house, didn't you?" Mary grinned at the detective. "I remember seeing them in your yard last year."

He looked pleased with himself. "You're right. I hadn't been in the mood to put them up this season, so they were just collecting dust in my garage. When Edna asked me to help her with this place, I thought I might as well bring everything to where there'll be kids to enjoy them."

Edna wondered if he might have gone to these extremes as a surprise for Starling. Could it be that her daughter's leaving for Colorado just before the holidays might have had something to do with Charlie's lack of enthusiasm for decorating his own house? These thoughts abruptly disappeared as her eyes fell again on the white truck's logo "Honeydew Home Repairs" and the stranger who walked forward from the vehicle. She eyed the man who looked to be about ten years older than Charlie. Early to mid-forties, she thought. What is an employee of Norm Wilkins doing at her home? Norm was the one person in the community who could set Edna's teeth to grinding.

*Don't be so unreasonable*, she scolded herself silently. Taking a step forward, she extended her hand. "Hello. I'm Edna Davies." The hostility she felt--and which she hoped didn't show on her face--began to fade as she tried to think of whom the man reminded her. "I'm guessing I have you to thank for helping Charlie decorate my home so beautifully."

"Kevin Lockhorn." He shook her hand with a firm but gentle grip. "I understand you knew my uncle, and I'm glad to help out."

Of course. She should have guessed immediately. He was heavier than Edna remembered Tom Greene to have been, but the dark curls were so much like his uncle's, even where they were beginning to go gray. With his charming smile and the twinkle in his eyes, the resemblance was such that Kevin could have been Tom's son.

"Yes, I did know your uncle, and I liked him

very much," Edna said, remembering with a pang that she had been a prime suspect in the man's murder. "How did you happen to get roped into this job?" She turned toward Charlie, frowning with the question as she remembered that Mary had told her about Tom's nephew moving to town to work for his cousin. Norm Wilkins was the owner of the handyman business, and Charlie knew full well what her feelings were about the man. She would never have hired one of Norm's employees to help put up the Christmas decorations. She refused to give Norm any of her business after the way he'd treated her when she'd been hunting for Tom's killer.

"Things were slow this morning, so I thought I'd come by and introduce myself." Kevin's words brought her back to the present. "Uncle Tom spoke highly of you." He paused briefly as if searching for the right words to continue. "I understand you helped solve his murder." He looked curiously at her as he voiced this thought. "I didn't see much of him in the years before he died, but we were still a close family."

"It was my fault," Charlie interrupted as he clapped a hand on Kevin's shoulder. "I corralled him."

Edna suspected the detective was trying to lighten everyone's mood and swing the conversation away from Tom and the murder. "Kevin happened to arrive at just the right time to help us raise and secure old Santa to the roof."

"Us?" Edna glanced around, wondering if another body or two would appear from the bushes.

"The other guys left about twenty minutes ago," Charlie said. "I called a couple of friends from the department who I knew weren't working this morning. I wanted to have everything done before you got back. If I'd known you were going to go shopping, we could have put up more lights and stuff. I've got a bunch of outdoor, baseball-sized ornaments I could hang around these yew trees."

Edna laughed with delight. "You did much more than I expected and a splendid job it is, too." *I do hope Albert will be as pleased as I am.* The thought flashed through her mind and was gone in an instant. Christmas was for children, and she knew their grandchildren, especially, were going to love this holiday spectacle.

"Want us to get your tree off the car?" It was Kevin who made the offer.

"Yes, please. That would be very helpful," Edna said, turning to him with a smile. "I'm about to make lunch for everyone. Can you stay?"

"I'd like to, ma'am, but I've probably been away from the office too long already. Norm was out on a job this morning. That's why I could get away at all."

"Can you join us for a tree-trimming party this evening, then?"

Kevin hesitated for only a second or two. "Yes, ma'am. I'd like that."

"Good," Mary spoke up. "I think you were about twenty, the last time I saw you. We have some catchin' up to do."

"And I'll enjoy hearing more about your family," Edna added her own enthusiasm.

The two men grappled the six-foot spruce tree off the roof of Mary's Jeep and set it in the stand Edna had put at the end of the living room. After that, Kevin left with a broad smile and an assurance that he was looking forward to helping decorate the evergreen that evening.

While Edna heated butternut squash soup and melted cheese on saltine crackers for lunch, Charlie hung the wreath on the front door. In the hall, Mary wrapped the evergreen rope around the newel post and up the banister to the second floor landing. Benjamin followed Mary up the stairs, occasionally attacking the swaying end of the rope.

By the time lunch was over and the kitchen cleaned up, it was almost two o'clock. Mary had gone home to take Hank and Spot out for a walk when Charlie announced his intention to go across the street to see if Gran was home. He still needed to ask her about bicycle sightings.

"I'll go with you," Edna said, draping the dish towel over the edge of the sink to dry. "I want to invite her to my party this evening."

Having become friends and visiting with their neighbor fairly often, Edna knew to walk up the driveway to the deck instead of ringing the front doorbell. Taking that route, they'd pass beneath the kitchen window where, if she were in her usual working mode, Gran would spot them on their way to the back door.

As they crossed the deck, Charlie was glancing down and around at the redwood planks. When Gran opened the kitchen door, he said, "Who's your visitor?"

She first gave Edna a brief welcoming hug before she frowned up at Charlie, clearly puzzled. "What visitor?"

He stood aside and, fixing his gaze on the boards of the deck, swept his arm back to indicate what he meant.

The sun had melted most of the storm's evidence of the night before, but where heavy boots had stepped and packed the snow, Edna now noticed that, indeed, someone had walked across the deck and stood at the kitchen window.

## Chapter 8

"Humph." Gran showed more puzzlement than worry. "Whoever it was must have come by before I got up this morning or when I was in the shower. People are always coming to the back door for one reason or another, even the postman brings packages around to the deck. Almost nobody uses the front. Everyone knows, if we're to home, Carol and I are here in the kitchen." The octogenarian stepped out onto the planking and studied the tracks, saying almost to herself, "I wonder who it was?" After several seconds, she shrugged, raised her head and smiled at her guests as if it were of no concern. "If it's important, they'll be back. Better come in before we let all the heat out." She turned and led the way into the house.

The kitchen was warm and smelled of baking bread and brewing coffee. Motioning Edna and Charlie to padded wood chairs at the white kitchen table immediately inside the door, Gran went to the counter and returned with three mugs. Short and plump, she was dressed in a calf-length, gray woolen skirt and a baby blue sweater set. Her white hair was neatly done up in a French twist at the back of her head, and her hazel eyes sparked with pleasure in welcoming company.

Wordlessly, Edna took a seat on the far side of

the table and looked across at Charlie. While Gran's back had been turned, Edna raised her eyebrows in silent question. Does Gran not realize the signs of a Peeping Tom? Whoever it was hadn't come to the door. They'd stood looking in at the window. Suddenly, she wished Carol were home. At least there'd be someone in the house with Gran … or was Gran safer with Carol gone? Edna's head began to throb.

When the older woman finally came to join them after adding a plate of frosted sugar cookies and a tea pot to the table, Charlie said, "Your visitor was here last night, not this morning after the sun was up."

Joanna Cravendorf, known to everyone as "Gran," had grown up in nearby Westerly. When her husband retired from Electric Boat, he insisted they move to Florida. After his death four years ago, she'd thought about returning to Rhode Island, but nothing had prompted her to take action until her granddaughter needed a place to hide this past year. The two women had planned it carefully, or so they'd thought. Gran would buy a house in her name. Since Carol had been born and raised in Illinois, and she didn't share her grandmother's name, nobody would think to look for her in Rhode Island. The criminal gang would have no way to trace Carol James if she didn't use credit cards or rent a place in her own name. To be on the safe side, however, Carol became "Jaycee Watkins" when she moved into the house across the street from the Davies. None of their plans had kept the thugs away for long.

Now, seated with Charlie and Edna at the kitchen table, Gran poured tea as she pondered what Charlie had just told her. After a moment's thought, she shrugged.

"Must have come after midnight, then. I was right here in the kitchen, baking until nearly twelve. After that, I went upstairs to bed and watched television for a while. Carol says I turn up the volume too loud." She wrinkled her nose, looking much like a mischievous gnome. "I probably do. Probably why I wouldn't hear if someone knocked on the window last night. I took my recipe box up with me for a little bedtime reading." Her face lit up when she added, "I'm making the soups at the restaurant tomorrow."

Although ostensibly only visiting from Thanksgiving through the New Year, Gran had quickly become reacquainted with old friends and, through one, had *assumed*, rather than been *given*, a part-time job at Krispin's Kitchen. The owner had been a childhood friend and neighbor of Gran's in Westerly.

"Have you heard from Carol?" Edna wanted to ease the conversation back to the mystery voyeur without appearing to be as alarmed as she felt.

"Yes indeed," The older woman brightened. "She called last night. Got to Chicago just fine. Says everything's going okay and she'll be home tomorrow or the day after."

"I'm concerned about those footsteps on the deck, Gran." Apparently, Charlie was thinking along the same lines as Edna. "It looks like he came only to look in the window, not knock on the door."

Gran frowned at the detective. "It could have been anyone. I told you, only strangers go to the front door. Everyone else comes to the back, including deliveries."

"But not in the middle of the night," he said.

"Now don't you go trying to scare me, young man. If you think you know who it was, spit it out. What are you trying to tell me?"

Edna put out her hand and patted Gran's forearm. "We're only guessing, Gran, but we wonder if someone might be looking for Carol. We don't want to frighten you, but we do want you to be aware of what might be going on."

"You mean those men who are on trial?" Gran looked from Edna to Charlie and shook her head in disbelief. "Why would they be after Carol? Everything she knows is on tape now. She's only in Chicago to answer a few last-minute questions."

"As Edna said, we're just guessing at this point." Charlie reached across the table to hold Gran's hand for a second. "We won't know for sure until we know who came to your house last night."

"Are you thinking someone might threaten me to get at Carol?" What they were suggesting finally seemed to be sinking in. Gran now looked worried. Edna was certain the concern would be for Carol and not for Gran herself.

Charlie shook his head. "I can't say what they might be up to." He frowned as he stared into his tea mug before raising his eyes to Gran's. "You're right about one thing. It doesn't make much sense, since everything your granddaughter knows about the arsonists has been captured in her photographs or is part of her sworn and videoed statement. The horse is already out of the barn, so to speak."

"I'll be so glad when that darn trial is over. Maybe then they'll leave Carol in peace." Gran's words came out through gritted teeth and her hands were clenched into fists but her eyes brimmed with unshed tears as she finally seemed to accept their warning.

"I'm sorry if I've alarmed you, but I don't think you're in serious danger." Charlie said. He reached over to squeeze her hand. "Whoever it was only looked in the window last night."

Edna wondered if the implication in Charlie's words would occur to Gran, that if the person had been serious about entering the house, he could have broken the window or forced the back door. She shuddered at the thought and returned her attention to what Charlie was saying.

"Carol is safe with the agents in Chicago, and we'll keep an eye on things around here. We'll catch your Peeping Tom. Just make sure to keep your doors and windows locked." He paused briefly before adding, "And you might want to pull down the shades after dark."

Still concerned for Gran's safety, isolated as the elderly woman was, Edna asked, "Did Carol leave her car with you or park at the airport?" She was remembering something she'd learned from a television program, and an idea formed in her mind.

"I have the car, so I can get back and forth to the diner. A friend drove Carol to the airport."

"Does her Kia have one of those remotes with a panic button?"

Gran thought briefly before nodding. "Yeeesss," she said hesitantly, obviously trying to understand what the question had to do with their recent conversation.

"Take the car keys upstairs when you go to bed and put them somewhere handy. Maybe under your pillow," Edna suggested. "If you hear someone trying to break in or if you think someone has gotten into the house, set off the car alarm. That should also make the lights flash, so keep the car in the driveway and not in the garage, at least until Carol comes home. In the off chance the noise and lights don't chase off an intruder, I or one of the other neighbors will hear the alarm and call nine-one-one."

Gran nodded and her expression brightened slightly. "That's a good idea. I'll do it."

"There's another thing," Charlie said. "In your comings and goings from the house, have you ever seen someone riding a bicycle in the neighborhood?"

"What a strange thing to ask," Gran said, picking up her tea mug to take a sip.

Charlie explained about the mysteriously moving bikes while Edna and Gran sipped tea and nibbled cookies. When he reached the last incident of the bicycle being found leaning against the dumpster at the new restaurant, Gran spoke up, her face alight with interest.

"That's my friend's diner. I'll ask Priscilla if she's heard any scuttlebutt from her customers."

"Priscilla?" Edna didn't recognize the name.

"Priscilla Powell. She's the manager at Krispin's

Kitchen, my friend's daughter." Mentioning the newest cafe in town made Gran's eyes sparkle. "Have you been there? Faye--that's my friend, Faye Krispin--her plan is to provide good, wholesome food at reasonable prices that students and pensioners can afford. I'm delighted she's letting me work there. A few of us are volunteers, you know. That's one reason she can keep prices down. For the first time in my life, I'm working for tips." She laughed at the idea.

"What do you do at the Kitchen?" Charlie asked.

Edna thought his question was aimed at keeping Gran from realizing the implications for her granddaughter, and she liked him for his sensitivity. She wondered anew if his relationship with Starling was cooling. She hoped not.

"Oh, I do a little of everything. Mostly I help out in the kitchen, but sometimes I wait tables for a few hours in the evenings, for the dinner crowd." She beamed with pride. "I'm even learning to run the cash register."

"Will you be working tonight?" Edna asked and hurried to explain. "I'm having a tree-trimming party this evening, and I'd be pleased if you could join us."

Without hesitation, Gran accepted. "I'm off today because I'll be working late tomorrow night. Priscilla's been invited to a Christmas party, so I've volunteered to lock up. I'd love to come to your party."

"Wonderful," Edna said before the thought of Gran locking up struck her. "Will you be alone at the diner tomorrow night?" she asked, glancing at

Charlie to see if he was as concerned as she felt.

"Oh, no. There's a handyman who sweeps up, washes dishes and does general odd jobs for his meals. I'm sure he'll be around," Gran's hazel eyes twinkled and the smile lines at the sides of her eyes and mouth deepened. "As a matter of fact, he's another old friend from my childhood," she said in voice that made her sound as coquettish as a schoolgirl.

"Oh?" Edna grinned at Gran's obvious pleasure.

"He's called Codfish," Gran confided to her audience. "Great name for an old fisherman, don't you think?"

Edna and Charlie agreed, happy for the widow. Edna, thinking how mysterious were the ways of Fate, wondered if Gran knew the history of her house's former owner and Codfish McKale.

Chapter 9

Edna and Charlie soon left Gran to her baking and returned to the Davies house to get ready for the party that evening. Charlie stayed long enough to help pull out Christmas decorations from among unpacked boxes in the basement and carry them upstairs. He promised to arrive half an hour earlier than everyone else that evening to string the tree lights.

Glancing at the clock, Edna thought she'd phone Albert before getting too wrapped up in party preparations. His doctor's appointment had been that morning, so besides wanting to hear his voice, she hoped to get the latest report on his knee.

"Hello, dear," he said, obviously having read the caller-id display before picking up.

"Hello yourself, sweetheart. How are you feeling?"

They chatted for a few minutes before Edna asked, "What did the doctor say this morning?"

With enthusiasm, Albert told her about the new leg brace he'd been given. It was adjustable, so he could begin to bend the knee and start the process of strengthening muscles again. She was happy to hear the optimism in his voice that he'd be "good as new in no time a' tall."

"With this increased mobility, I can probably get

Roger to drive me home tomorrow."

Not wishing to quash Albert's excitement, Edna said, "It'll be best if they bring you home when you all come down for Mary's Christmas Eve open house. It's only three more days, dear." She thought of something that might help to cheer him up. "Starling and Grant will be flying in that day. If there's enough room in the rental with Karissa and the children, maybe you can drive down a little early with them."

She was relieved when Albert seemed to accept the plan. "Good idea. I'll call Grant as soon as we hang up." After a brief pause, he said, "You're probably right about my staying with Diane, too. I have another checkup day after tomorrow, so it will be best if I stay here a couple more nights."

They chatted for a few minutes longer before Edna promised to phone again the next evening and rang off. In the kitchen, she turned the radio to an all-music holiday station before making unadorned popcorn and putting whole, fresh cranberries into a bowl, ready for stringing with needle and thread. One of her favorite traditions was the red and white garland for wrapping around the tree until the day after Christmas when it would be hung outside for the birds to enjoy.

She put a dozen eggs in a pan to boil while she prepared a dip with equal parts cream cheese and mayonnaise, along with thyme, garlic powder and freshly ground pepper. She cut celery and carrots into strips and arranged them on a plate with an assortment of crackers to accompany the bowl of herb mix. Finally, before going upstairs to don her red velour pants suit, she searched through the Christmas boxes for the special tin-lined pot she used to make her grandmother's mulled wine recipe. Her grandmother insisted that the pot be used for nothing else or it might add unwanted flavors to her favorite holiday beverage.

Shortly before her guests were to arrive, Edna deviled the eggs, mulled the wine and heated cider. As she was making these last-minute preparations, she began to wonder why Charlie hadn't shown up. The time-consuming job of untangling and stringing the lights around the tree would delay the rest of the decorating.

She forced her mind to other things. Anticipating with pleasure the arrival of Tom's nephew, she remembered a special gift she could cross off her list. Searching the closet where her paints were stored, she found the portrait of Tom Greene she'd sketched shortly after the handyman's death. She studied his face, thinking as she did so, *I wish you could be with us this evening.*

Rummaging in her office cupboards, she found a cardboard tube she'd saved from a roll of heavy-duty aluminum foil. Cutting the cylinder to the width of the sketch paper, she then rolled the portrait and slid it into the tube before wrapping it with red Christmas paper. She added a green bow and a small note "To Danny" and leaned the package against the wall behind the tree. Still Charlie hadn't arrived.

When she looked at the clock, Edna realized that Mary should have been there by now, too. Usually, she was early rather than late to Edna's parties.

"I wonder where everybody is," Edna muttered to Benjamin, seconds before the doorbell rang.

Greatly relieved, she hurried down the hall, knowing it would be Charlie. Mary always let herself in through the mudroom. Edna's heart sank when she flung the door wide--nearly calling "Where have you been?"--only to see Gran standing on the stoop with a bowl of homemade chocolate turtles in her hands.

*Where was Charlie,* Edna wondered, beginning to feel anxious that she hadn't heard from him.

"Am I too early?" Gran brought Edna out of her trance by handing her the bowl and pushing past her. "Brrr. It's getting mighty cold. They're saying it might drop below zero tonight." When Edna didn't respond, Gran turned back to look at her with a quizzical frown. "Is something the matter?"

"Not at all," Edna assured her, trying to smile and hide her concern. She mentally shook herself to clear her mind and began again. "I mean, no, you're not too early and yes, something is wrong. Charlie isn't here and the lights haven't been strung yet. I also expected Mary to be here by now, but you're the first to arrive. I'm sure everything is fine and they've just forgotten the time."

"Well, let's go see what we can do about those lights."

Gran's cheerful, take-charge command was what Edna needed to snap out of her funk. She led the way to the living room where Benjamin scurried before them to jump into his bed by the hearth near a low fire. Edna had put Christmas discs in the player and Nat King Cole was singing "Deck the

Halls" as they entered the room. The women had just begun to untangle strings of lights when the doorbell rang again.

"Happy holiday," Kevin said, handing Edna a bouquet of red roses and white lilies when she opened the door.

She was again struck by how much the man resembled his uncle.

"Merry Christmas," Gran greeted as she walked up behind Edna to meet the new arrival.

"Happy holidays," he replied, unzipping his parka.

Gran looked at Edna with raised eyebrows. "Doesn't anyone say 'Merry Christmas' anymore?"

Before she could answer, Kevin said. "It's not politically correct these days." His smile didn't reach his eyes, and Edna couldn't tell if he was talking with tongue in cheek or not.

Apparently, Gran chose to think *not*. "I'm sorry, young man, but it's just as 'P.C.' as saying 'Happy holidays.' Perhaps more so." Gran's tone was gentle but firm. "Do you know why?" Edna could tell that Gran was about to tell them, regardless of their answers.

"Christmas," the elderly woman continued without waiting for a reply, "is the celebration of the birth of the Christ Child, which is why it is called 'Christmas.' It is also a federal holiday, signed into law by President Ulysses S. Grant in eighteen-seventy, so even if you're not of a faith that worships Jesus, it is still right and proper to celebrate 'Christmas' as a holiday and refer to it as such." She smiled, giving Kevin a nod as if pleased to have shared her knowledge. "Now, do you think there's something wrong with that?"

Having dropped his jacket onto a nearby chair, Kevin grimaced playfully and threw up his hands in mock surrender. "I give up. You're right. It's 'Merry Christmas' for me from now on."

Slightly uncomfortable with his exaggerated capitulation, Edna urged her guests toward the living room.

Kevin volunteered to string the lights, and Edna helped by untangling the cords. Gran said she'd make the garland and went to sit in Edna's wingback chair near the fire to string popcorn and cranberries while she softly hummed along with the carols.

"You must be used to cold winters, coming from Michigan," Edna said, wanting to put Kevin at ease.

"No, ma'am. Not used to it at all. I moved up here from Texas."

Edna was confused. "I guess I misunderstood. I thought you grew up in Michigan."

He smiled as he walked around the tree, pinning lights along the branches. "I did, but I joined the army right out of high school, traveled around a bit and ended up at Fort Hood. After twenty-five years, I figured enough was enough, so I took my walking papers. After my discharge, I decided to see something of the state before heading back to the U.P."

When he paused to plug the next string of lights onto the chain, Edna asked, "Yoo-pea?"

"That's what we call the northern part of Michigan, the Upper Peninsula. Yes, ma'am, I'm a

Yooper, or at least I was until I joined the army."

"And you stayed in Texas after you left the service?" Edna enjoyed hearing about the travels of others, curious now whether Kevin moved to Rhode Island purely to work for his cousin.

"Yes, ma'am. I traveled around the state some, working odd jobs. I'm a country boy, so I took ranch jobs instead of heading for the cities. When Cousin Norm offered to make me a partner in his business, I thought it might be nice to live near family. I haven't been in this part of the country since I was in high school, but I remember Uncle Tom's farm and how pretty it was here in the fall."

"You finished with those lights?" Gran came up to the tree, holding up her popcorn and cranberry garland, effectively ending the conversation.

While Kevin obligingly threaded the garland around the upper branches, Edna and Gran opened boxes and bags of ornaments. Edna's favorites were the gold medallions for the members of her family, each with the person's name and date of birth.

"Albert and I started the tradition when Diane, our second, was born," she explained to Gran. "We began with the four of us that year and now we're four times that many with our children's spouses and children." She added with a burst of happiness, "We'll all be together this Christmas for the first time in three years."

Finished hanging the garland, Kevin walked over to join them. "My dad used to wake me on Christmas Eve by stomping on the roof of our house." When Edna and Gran stopped what they were doing to look at him expectantly, he went on,

"After Mom put presents under the tree and filled stockings, she was ready to go to bed, but he'd get out the ladder and climb up on the roof. Most likely, he'd had a toddy or two by that time. Years later, Mom told me how she'd have to go out in the cold to help him off the roof and down the ladder. Said she always expected him to fall off and break his neck." Kevin finished with a laugh.

Thinking it wasn't the most pleasant tradition she'd ever heard, Edna nonetheless gave a cheerful chuckle and changed the conversation around to Tom Greene's grandson. "Do you know if Danny still believes in Santa Claus?" She approached the tree carrying several wooden ornaments in her hands.

"If he does, this will be the last year," Kevin said, following after Edna to hang a tiny elf figure on a low branch. "There'll be at least one of his classmates in the first grade who'll tell him the real scoop."

"I suppose you're right," she said, hooking a carved reindeer over a middle branch. "It's such fun when the children still believe, though."

"That's what Cousin Norm thinks too. He's going to dress up as Santa one more year, whether Danny believes or not." As he spoke, Kevin wandered over to the coffee table to eat a few crackers and drink some cider.

Proud of her grandmother's holiday drink, Edna said, "Would you like to try some mulled wine?"

He shook his head. "Cider's fine. Alcohol doesn't agree with me, or I don't agree with it. Tried for years, but never figured out which." He smiled and popped a cracker into his mouth.

Before Edna had time to think of what he meant, Kevin went on with his story.

"It's part of a family tradition. Norm gets into costume and goes over to the house to tuck Danny into bed. Because Norm had no children of his own, Uncle Tom thought up the idea for Danny's first Christmas."

"Norm?" Edna couldn't believe the meanest man she'd ever known would be capable of such an act. "Norm Wilkins?" she repeated as a question, just to make certain she understood that she and Kevin were talking about the same person.

"Yep. That's right." Kevin laughed. "Hard to believe, I know, but he loves playing Santa Claus. He's a different person when he's dressed in that red suit. He's actually really good with kids and animals. Did you know he poses as Santa for pet photos at a local animal clinic?"

Edna remembered with a start the fat Santa who had arrived at Laurel Taylor's shelter with Jake Perry. *No wonder those beady eyes and sour expression looked familiar,* she thought. Catching sight of the clock, she was distracted and amazed to see nearly two hours had slipped by.

Gran must have seen the look. "What do you suppose has happened to Charlie and Mary?" she asked. While Kevin and Edna had been talking, Gran had returned to her chair to thread another garland which she now held up to Kevin.

"He mentioned the department was short staffed. Maybe he got called in on a case," Edna said, beginning to drape tinsel over the decorated branches and trying not to look as worried as she felt. "I don't know what could be keeping Mary, though, or why she hasn't called."

As if her last words were some sort of signal, the phone rang. Startled by the coincidence, Edna took a second or two to realize it really was her phone ringing, but then she raced to her office.

"Sorry I'm missing the party, Edna." Charlie said as soon as she picked up. Breathless from hurrying, she didn't respond immediately, so he said, "Is Mary still there? I need to speak to her."

"No. She's missing the party, too. What's going on, Charlie?"

There was a brief pause on the line before she heard him sigh. "Laurel Taylor's dead. One of the volunteers found her and phoned it in."

"How? When?" Edna realized she was babbling, shocked by the news.

"I'm sorry to break it to you like this. I would have driven over to tell you, but I'm at the scene and I need to talk to Mary."

For the moment, Edna ignored his request since she obviously couldn't conjure Mary out of thin air. Instead, she said, "What happened?"

"Looks like she fell down the stairs. She might have tried to grab the railing, but only caught the evergreen rope. It's been ripped away from the banister. Glass Christmas balls are shattered all over the floor in the hallway. I thought at first it might have been an accident, but now I'm not so sure. I found mistletoe in her teapot. It's a small sprig, but there are berries on it. I know the berries are the most poisonous part, but I don't know if the amount in the tea was enough to kill her. I'm thinking maybe it made her sick and she decided to go upstairs to lie down. Maybe she tripped or fainted at the top of the staircase and fell backwards. The medical examiner's going to have to confirm cause of death."

Edna remembered what Mary had said about Laurel's brewing habits. Microwaving the teapot with mistletoe berries in it would certainly have poisoned the water. Thinking of Laurel, Edna recalled an image of the woman rolling her eyes and grinning as she held a twig of mistletoe over her head. She wouldn't have poisoned her own tea, would she?

Charlie's voice broke into her thoughts. "You say Mary's not there. Do you know where she is?"

"No. She never showed up. Kevin Lockhorn and Gran are the only ones here."

"You haven't heard from her?"

"Not a word."

"That's strange," Charlie didn't speak again for several seconds. Edna waited. Finally, he said, "One of Laurel's neighbors saw Mary backing out of the driveway at CATS this afternoon. He thinks it was around four or four-thirty. Said Mary took off, burnin' rubber. That's not like her either. I've tried phoning her, but she doesn't pick up. Her machine isn't on at her home number, but I left a message on her cell to call me back, in case I didn't reach her at your place."

"Like I said, she never showed up and I haven't heard from her." Edna's mind was racing, trying to think why Mary might have gone back to Laurel's or where she could be now when she should have been at Edna's party. "Was anyone else at Laurel's house this afternoon besides Mary? The volunteers must come and go. You don't think Mary had anything to do with Laurel's death, do you?"

"Can't say until I talk to her," he said. "And, yes, there were other people in and out of the house today. I'm trying to get a handle on who was here and when."

"I was at the shelter this morning with Mary. Maybe I can answer some of your questions."

"I understand Doctor Jake and someone in a Santa Claus costume were here in the morning, taking pictures. Roselyn Perry stopped by, too, probably around lunchtime or shortly after. I think maybe a young college student named Bethany was here in the afternoon, shortly before or just after Mary, but the neighbors can't seem to agree on the time."

"Mary and I left CATS when Jake arrived with Santa, but Roselyn wasn't with them." Edna thought back to the morning. "An older woman was leaving when Mary and I arrived at the house. She was pretty angry. We heard her say something about Laurel going to be sorry. She was driving a bright blue car, license ending in three two. I couldn't tell you the make. It was small, a compact, if that's any help."

"Thanks. I'll get someone to follow up on that. I want to talk with anyone who was in the house." There was a pause on the line, and Edna imagined Charlie was writing notes to himself. Eventually, he said, "I guess I've got enough information for now.

I'll see if I can reach Doctor Jake. He may be able to give me more names, or a timeline on when he was there. So far, it sounds like Mary might have been the last to arrive and leave, but I'm not yet sure about the college student. That's why I particularly want to talk to her, to both of them," he amended.

"Did you know that Norm Wilkins is the Santa who works with Jake?"

Charlie guffawed. "You're kidding." He laughed again. "He's got the belly for it, but I'm not sure about the disposition. Can't imagine his eyes twinkling, although he's got the red nose."

Edna couldn't help smiling at the same disbelief she'd felt over the news, but sobered quickly. "Shall I go over and see if Mary's home? Maybe she's had an accident. If she hasn't been home, I should check on Hank and Spot." Her mind raced over the possibility of Mary lying hurt, or worse, in her house.

"No. Thanks, Edna. I'll send a patrol car over. Meanwhile, if you hear from her, have her call me, would you?"

"Yes, and you do the same. Let me know as soon as you hear anything."

Before Charlie could hang up, Edna asked, "What about the cats? What will happen to Laurel's cats?"

"I've got an animal control officer coming over to round them up. Do you know how many are in the house? I've seen four, but I don't know if others might be hiding."

"Four is correct. Let me know if I can do

anything. I suppose we'll have to find homes for them. Snowflake is the white one. She's deaf. She needs to be kept with the black cat. His name is Charcoal."

"Okay. I'll pass the word."

Edna had been standing with her back to the office door. As she hung up and turned around, she was startled to see Kevin leaning against the doorjamb.

"Everything okay?" he asked before she could catch her breath. "You were gone so long, I thought I'd come check on you."

Edna wondered how long he'd been standing there. How much had he overheard? Aloud, she said, "I'm afraid everything is not okay. A woman I met recently has been found dead."

"Who?" he asked, still blocking the doorway.

Thinking he might know her through his work at Honeydew Home Repairs, Edna said, "Laurel Taylor. She runs a cat shelter about a mile northwest of town."

Kevin took a step backwards as if one of his knees had just given out. He also looked a little pale, Edna thought, as she took a step toward him. "Are you okay?" she asked, but before he could answer, Gran appeared in the hall.

She seemed not to notice Kevin's distress as she slipped past him to enter the room. "Has something happened? Anything wrong?" The older woman studied Edna's face.

By that time, Kevin seemed to have regained himself, and Edna felt suddenly weary. "I've just received some shocking news, and I'm feeling a bit shaky."

"What can I do to help?" Gran asked.

"Maybe you'd like to be alone," Kevin suggested.

Edna nodded. "I'm sorry to break up the party, but I think that would be best. Please don't bother with anything. I'll clean up later, but first, I want to sit for a minute."

Gran would have protested, but Kevin took charge. Pulling out the desk chair, he steadied it for Edna to sit. When Gran offered to bring her some mulled wine or hot cider, he interrupted and insisted on escorting her home.

Grateful to the man, Edna sat numbly and listened to the sounds of her guests as they retrieved their coats and left. A few minutes after hearing the front door close, she reached for the phone and dialed Mary's home number. Letting it ring a dozen times, she finally hung up when neither Mary nor her answering machine picked up.

After replacing the receiver in its cradle, she went to the mudroom and opened the side door to look over at Mary's house. She wanted to see if any lights were on, but when she opened the door, all she saw was white. Through heavily falling snow, she could barely make out the stone wall that marked the boundary between their two properties. As she stood, almost mesmerized by the whiteness, her thoughts drifted from Mary to Laurel. In her mind's eye, Edna saw a woozy Laurel falling backwards down the stairs, and suddenly doubt assailed her. Did Laurel fall or had she been pushed?

Chapter 10

Edna slept badly that night. First, she wondered what could have happened to Mary. Thinking about her neighbor having been seen speeding away from CATS, Edna's thoughts turned to Laurel Taylor, and then it was like an old phonograph needle stuck in a groove. Around and around her mind turned on the woman she'd met so recently. Did the woman fall or had she been pushed down the stairs? What about the mistletoe? Had someone poisoned Laurel or had she done that to herself? Would she have been foolish enough to put mistletoe into her own teapot? If so, was it pure ignorance or had she planned to serve a toxic brew to someone else? Edna realized she had developed a suspicious nature since she'd run up against more than one murderer, but she couldn't keep her mind from exploring the possibilities.

At six the next morning, knowing she wouldn't get any more sleep, she got out of bed and went to the window. The storm hadn't been as bad as predicted nor, apparently, had it continued to fall as heavily as last night. She estimated the accumulation to be about six inches, but looking up at the sky, she was certain there would be more before the day was over. She would have to find someone to shovel her driveway. Charlie might oblige, but she didn't feel she could bother him now that he was back at work. Someone to plow her out. Another item to add to my list, she thought.

On her way downstairs, each tread seemed to represent something she had yet to complete. *Make up the guest beds, clean the bathrooms and lay out fresh towels, check food supplies, finish writing and addressing Christmas cards.* Her steps faltered and her shoulders sagged.

In the kitchen, she had appetite only for a single muffin and a cup of coffee for breakfast, usually her best meal of the day. Swallowing the last drops in her cup, she decided not to wait for a decent hour to phone Mary. Edna had not heard from Charlie, and she needed to know that all was well next door.

Still, there was no answer. She hung up when the machine kicked in, deciding to try Mary's cell phone. She didn't know why she hadn't tried that number the previous evening, but she dialed it now. Hearing Mary's curt "Leave a message" voice recording, Edna requested an immediate call-back before hanging up in bewilderment. Where was Mary and why wasn't she answering her phones?

Housebound until she could get plowed out, Edna decided to work in her office and get a few Christmas cards out of the way. That would cheer her somewhat and distract her from all the questions spinning around in her head. She should get some of the housecleaning done, but she wanted to be close to the phone in case someone called. As it happened, she hadn't even had a chance to sit down when the phone rang. The caller wasn't whom Edna expected, at least not before eight o'clock.

"Mornin', Edna," Gran greeted. "Heard anything from Mary?"

"Hello, Gran. No, not a word yet." Doubtful that Mary was foremost on the old woman's mind, Edna said, "You're up early."

"Yes, well, that's why I'm phoning. I need a great favor from you."

Edna looked at the stack of cards she hadn't even begun to address. "Okay," she said with some hesitation and a sinking feeling in her stomach.

If Gran detected the reluctance Edna felt, she ignored it. "Codfish called this morning. Woke me up to say that Laurel Taylor is dead. Do you know her? She runs a cat shelter."

Hadn't Gran heard the news last night? Realization flicked through Edna's mind that Gran had still been in the living room when she'd told Kevin the gist of Charlie's call. Kevin must not have mentioned the fatality to Gran when he escorted her across the street.

Aloud, Edna said, "I met her this past week, as a matter of fact. Terrible tragedy. That was why Charlie phoned last night, why he wasn't able to come to the party." Remembering that Gran had been away from Rhode Island for years and that Laurel was fairly new to town, Edna asked, "How do you know Laurel?"

"I don't … or *didn't*, I should say. Never met the woman, but I spoke to her on the phone. My friend Codfish's nephew put me in touch with her when I mentioned I wanted to get a kitten for Carol. As a Christmas present, you know. I was supposed to pick up the kitty from her today at the shelter."

"The police have probably relocated the cats by this time. Have you called the station?"

"No. That's why I'm calling you. Codfish said Roselyn from Perry's Animal Clinic is going over to collect the cats this morning. He said she'd be at Laurel's house early, before she has to open the clinic. That's why he called me so early, so I can meet her at CATS."

"The police didn't take them away last night?" Edna was certain that Charlie had said he'd contacted the animal control unit.

"Apparently, all the shelters are full. There was no place to take them last night, so someone contacted the Perrys. That's what Codfish told me. The cats will stay at the clinic, but only for a few days. If homes aren't found for them, they'll have to be put down."

"I'm still not certain what you want me to do. Do you want me to adopt one of Laurel's cats?"

"Oh, no," Gran chuckled. "That won't be necessary … at least, I don't think it will be. I'd like you to drive me to CATS so I can pick up the kitten. I haven't even seen the little calico yet. I arranged everything with Laurel by phone so Carol wouldn't suspect anything before Christmas. I thought I'd have to spoil the surprise by having her drive me to the shelter, so her unplanned trip to Chicago was a blessing of sorts. I was going to drive over this morning to pick up the little calico. Carol says her Kia handles beautifully in this weather, but I'm not used to driving in the snow anymore. That's why I was wondering if you'd be so kind …"

Finally realizing what Gran was asking of her,

Edna decided that going to CATS might give her an opportunity to learn something more about Laurel's death and maybe provide a clue as to what might have happened to Mary. "Of course," Edna said, her mind quickly reshuffling her day's schedule. "I'll drive you to the shelter, but first I need to arrange for someone to plow my driveway. There's too much snow for my car to push through. I wouldn't want to get stuck halfway around the circle."

"Oh, but we have to go soon." Gran sounded urgent. "The cats are probably being taken away right now, and I must be at the restaurant later this morning to start making the soups. Somebody already cleaned off my driveway this morning--I suspect Codfish had something to do with that." Edna caught the distinct pleasure in Gran's voice before the older woman went on more somberly, "The road has been plowed, too." When Edna didn't answer at once, Gran said, "You could drive the Kia." After another brief pause, she said, "Would now be a good time to go?"

The discussion about CATS had started Edna wondering why Mary had gone back to the shelter the previous afternoon. Gran's question snapped her back to the present problem. "I suppose I can go now. If we're to use Carol's car, I'll walk over to your place. Give me ten minutes."

"Oh, thank you, Edna. You're such a good neighbor." Gran hurried on as if she were afraid Edna might change her mind. "I'll go warm up the car."

The town road crews were out, clearing and sanding as quickly as they could, so driving wasn't as treacherous as Edna had feared. She drove slowly and was able to pull into Laurel's driveway, parking behind a white van. "Perry Animal Clinic" was printed on the back in large black letters, along with a phone number and a web site address. In front of the van was a patrol car.

"What a funny-looking little house," Gran exclaimed, staring at the gingerbread-adorned building that almost looked like only half a house. "It's unusual to see the front door so far over to one side."

"It is a little strange," Edna agreed. "Inside, all the rooms are off to the left."

Gran laughed. "That's one thing I like about older neighborhoods, so many of the houses were uniquely built. No problem mistaking your neighbor's house for your own like some of the modern communities."

"Shall we go in?" Edna was beginning to get cold. She enjoyed the octogenarian, but Gran tended to get side-tracked. Edna sometimes wondered if Gran needed to talk while she had an audience before going back to her single life in Florida.

Knowing someone from both the police department and Jake's clinic were already in the house, Edna didn't bother to knock or ring the bell. Instead, she opened the door and stuck her head in. "Hallooo," she called. "May we come in?"

Without waiting for an answer, she stepped over the threshold with Gran close on her heels. Remembering what Charlie had said about the Christmas balls shattered and scattered over the hallway, Edna saw that someone had swept them aside, probably so they wouldn't be ground into the wood floor under trampling boots. The evergreen garland, too, was lying beside the staircase with the broken glass. Edna shivered as she imagined Laurel trying to stop her fall by grabbing onto the flimsy boa. She glanced up at the light fixture where Mary had hung mistletoe and was surprised to see that a dangling bit of red ribbon was all that remained. Only the broad, red ribbons with their festive greeting cards still decorated the wall, undisturbed by whatever had happened. Two canvas animal carriers sat at the foot of the stairs. Edna could see Charcoal and Snowflake huddled together in one.

"Hi." A woman in police uniform walked down the hall from the kitchen, announcing her presence. "This house is restricted for the time being. Can I help you with something?"

At that same moment, Roselyn appeared at the top of the staircase holding a kitten in the crook of her arm. As she descended, an older, long-haired cat scampered down beside her. Edna thought she recognized the markings of a Maine Coon, one of the prettiest and smartest of the domestic felines. She must be the one Laurel had named "Auntie Bea."

So as not to snub the authority in charge of the house, Edna introduced herself and Gran before tipping her head toward Roselyn. "We've come to pick up the kitten. Mrs. Cravendorf has adopted her. We heard the shelters are full, so we thought we'd come over and take her off your hands."

While Edna was explaining their presence to the police officer, Gran had rushed forward to meet the veterinarian's wife at the bottom of the stairs. "Is that our Callie," she cooed, holding out her hands to take the kitten. The orange and black splashes of color on its mostly white body distinctly marked the tiny feline as both a calico and a female.

Roselyn shied and turned from Gran at the same time as she spoke to the patrol woman. "This is the lot. Laurel had only four in the house." She spoke quietly, keeping her head down and her attention focused on the cats now in her care.

Roselyn was tall with an athlete's build. She was a plain-looking woman who wore little or no makeup, and looked younger than her thirty-something years with her shiny brown hair pulled into a careless ponytail. Wisps of stray, straight strands had been tucked behind one ear. Edna's artistic assessment of the woman's features was interrupted by Gran speaking to the woman.

"I'm Joanna Cravendorf. I'd already arranged everything with Mrs. Taylor to get the kitten this morning."

Roselyn spoke softly, as if to the bundle in her arm, "The cats will have to go to the clinic first. They can be adopted out from there." Still she didn't look at the other women, but bent and gently placed her small charge into the empty carrier. As soon as she did so, Auntie Bea scooted in and sat crosswise between the door and the kitten, as if to protect the little one.

"Can we follow you to the clinic? You see, Callie is a Christmas present for my granddaughter and I'd like her to get used to the house before Carol--that's my granddaughter--before she gets home from Chicago. I must go to work this morning and I don't want to impose on my friend ..." Gran would have prattled on, but the police woman spoke up, stopping the flood of information Gran was offering.

"The Perrys must check the cats, make certain they're healthy and have all their shots. They have to follow procedures and fill out the paperwork. I'm sorry but you'll have to arrange to pick up your kitten at another time."

While the officer explained the process to Gran, Roselyn secured the latches on the carrier doors. In the past year of taking Benjamin to Perry's Animal Clinic, Edna had met the woman only once, learning from Mary that the veterinarian's wife was painfully shy. Her main responsibility was taking care of the animals they were boarding for longer than a few hours. The kennels that housed the animals at the back of the main office and surgery were Roselyn's domain.

She was still tending to the carriers when the policewoman stepped up to Gran. Extending an arm like a barrier, she gently herded the elderly woman back toward Edna and the front door. "As I said before, this is a restricted area. We're here this morning only to get the cats. I must ask you to leave now. We'll be heading out shortly ourselves." The uniformed woman smiled as if to soften any implied reprimand.

While she had the chance, Edna spoke quickly. "Roselyn, have you seen Mary or heard from her?"

The veterinarian's wife stood, lifting both carriers, but didn't turn around. Edna wondered if

Roselyn had even heard the question, but before she could repeat it, the policewoman hustled Edna and Gran out onto the porch. "You need to move your car. We'll be right behind you." She was still smiling when she shut the door behind them.

Edna took hold of Gran's arm as they trudged slowly through the snow back to the Kia. Once inside with seat belts fastened, Gran said, "I'm sorry, Edna. This has been a disappointing and wasted trip." She sounded dejected. "I don't know when I'll be able to pick up our kitten before Carol gets home. She's due to fly in tomorrow afternoon."

Edna was only vaguely aware of Gran's chatter as she continued to wonder what could have happened to Mary. Were Hank and Spot with her? Edna couldn't imagine Mary neglecting her pets. Surely, Roselyn or Jake must have heard from Mary.

"Edna?" Gran's persistent and loud calling of her name startled Edna.

"Sorry, Gran, I was thinking about our missing neighbor. What were you saying?"

"I asked if you wouldn't mind stopping at Krispin's on the way home. It's only a block or two out of the way. I'd like to check that Priscilla has all the supplies I need for making soup today."

With her thoughts now turned on all she had to do, but not knowing how to say no, Edna agreed. Beginning to feel very anxious about her friend, she couldn't get Mary off her mind, either. This disappearance wasn't like her. Where could she be and why hadn't she been in contact? Her big Christmas Eve open house was only two days away, the day Edna's own children and grandchildren were scheduled to fly in from Colorado. She glanced at the overcast and darkening sky. The snow had begun to fall again.

Chapter 11

Krispin's Kitchen closed between breakfast and lunch, so Gran dug in her purse and pulled out a key to the front door. The sidewalk had been shoveled and sprinkled with a mixture of sand and snowmelt, but already, newly fallen snow dusted the pavement. Whoever had cleared the walk had also been kind enough to remove the mound of snow left by the street plows, so Edna was able to park in front of the building.

Sleigh bells hanging on the back of the door clanged and jingled their arrival. The long, narrow diner was warm and smelled of percolating coffee. A counter ran along the right-hand side with a cash register at the near end. Beneath the register, a glass case displayed an assortment of locally made jewelry and other small craft items. Behind the counter, a pass-through offered a view into the kitchen.

Eight bar stools were lined up along the counter. Four booths occupied the left-hand wall and six square tables filled the middle of the room, leaving just enough space for servers to squeeze by. Edna's first impression of the small restaurant was that it was welcoming.

Christmas decorations were homemade and minimal but clever. Wreaths of green construction paper surrounded the portholes in the double, swinging doors to the kitchen. Pasted above the pass-through window, a cardboard cut-out sleigh, pulled by eight reindeer and led by a red-nosed Rudolph, slanted upward toward the ceiling. The jolly man holding the reins waved at the room while gaily wrapped presents spilled from an overloaded bag into the bed of the large sled. The only other decoration that caught Edna's eye was a green ceramic tree, complete with tiny, multi-colored lights, sitting on the far side of the old-fashioned cash register. A young man was sitting at a back table finishing his breakfast. Edna guessed he was the one who had cleared the walk.

"Hi, Vinnie," Gran called, raising a hand in greeting as she walked to the far end of the counter and disappeared through swinging doors into the room beyond, leaving Edna alone with the stranger.

"Vinnie?"

Although it was a thought she'd spoken aloud, he answered. "Yes, ma'am. Vinnie Valmont at your service." He rose and pulled out a chair, inviting her to join him. "Like a cup of coffee?"

"I'd love a coffee regular, please." Edna replied as she removed her coat and draped it over a nearby chair before sitting. The room was warm and felt good after the bitter cold of the outside.

He picked up his thick, white porcelain mug and headed for a set of glass pots on the warming burners behind the counter. One pot had a black spout, the other was orange.

"Here you are," he said on his return, "coffee with cream. Hope half and half is okay." He set the mug on the table in front of her before resuming his own seat.

"Perfect. Thank you." She wrapped her hands around the hot cup and introduced herself.

He grinned at her, raising his eyebrows. "You're Mary Osbourne's neighbor, aren't you?"

She laughed in surprise. "Now, how do you know that?"

"Tell you in a minute, but I have a question first. I'm having an argument with one of the customers about 'coffee regular'."

Edna lifted her cup, took a sip, and waited for Vinnie to continue.

"He's from New York and says that when he asks for 'a regular,' he gets coffee with cream and two sugars."

She thought for a minute, pulling a memory from her past. "When my brother was in the army, away from home for the first time, he learned fast that 'regular' means different things in different parts of the country. For some, it means both cream and sugar and for others, particularly in the south and west, it means 'black and caffeinated.' In Rhode Island, we mean 'cream, no sugar' I think, because sugar is on the table along with salt, pepper and other condiments--or it used to be when I was a girl. Not the packets they have today, but real sugar in glass jars with stainless steel lids. Cream wasn't left on the table because it would spoil."

"Hmmm," Vinnie said, taking a drink from his own mug. "The only sense all that makes is, I'd better ask each customer what he means when he orders 'regular' coffee."

"That would be safest." Edna laughed at his lopsided grin. "Now, will you tell me how you know I'm Mary's neighbor?"

"Friend of mine mentioned you yesterday. Said you and Mary were going to get our back pay from Laurel Taylor."

Edna nearly choked on the coffee she'd just sipped. Remembering the conversation in Mary's kitchen from two days ago, she said, "You're talking about Bethany Marco, if I'm not mistaken." When he nodded, she went on. "I hope you hadn't gotten your hopes up."

Leaning his forearms on the table with his own cup between his hands, Vinnie lowered his head to stare into the dark liquid, so Edna couldn't see his expression when he said, "Yeah, I heard. The wicked witch is dead."

A bit shocked by the disrespect of his comment, she marveled at the speed of communications in small communities. "How did you hear?"

He sat back in his chair, finally looking at her. "Bethany told me when I drove her to Kingston Station last night."

Edna thought quickly. Laurel had been found late yesterday afternoon. How had Bethany learned of it? Had she spoken to Mary? "What time did you take her to the station?"

He frowned as if puzzled by the question, but answered without hesitation. "A little after six. She caught the six forty-seven to Boston."

Mary was seen leaving CATS at four-thirty and Bethany tells Vinnie about Laurel less than two hours later. How did she know so fast? Thinking about it, Edna thought it might have been the volunteer who found Laurel. She probably would have been on the phone to anyone else who worked or had worked at the shelter. Bethany told Vinnie who told Codfish who phoned Gran. *And so on, and so on*, Edna thought and would have smiled at the speed of small-town grapevines except for the seriousness of the event.

"One of the neighbors saw Bethany ride her bike up to Laurel's house yesterday afternoon." If Vinnie wondered where she had heard this news, he kept silent, so she went on, hoping to stir a response. "I'm surprised she went back after the way Laurel treated her."

He shrugged and looked away from her toward the view into the kitchen. "Bethany gets impatient about things. She said she hadn't heard from Mary, so she decided to go see Laurel herself."

"I thought she didn't want to speak to Laurel ever again. That's why she asked Mary and me to go."

He turned back to face her with another shrug. "What can I say? I sure don't understand women." His smile was crooked, as if in apology.

"How did she know we hadn't already gotten the money for her?" Edna felt a flash of irritation toward the young woman. If Bethany was able to speak to Laurel herself, why had she sent Mary and Edna to intercede for her? *A waste of my time*, Edna thought before her ire was replaced by a surge of hope. "Was she finally able to talk to Mary yesterday afternoon? Is that how she knew about Laurel's death?"

He shook his head. "I don't know. All she told me was that she went over there to get what was owed her. The train ticket tapped her out, and she needed cash for Christmas."

"Was it a last-minute decision?" Edna asked, "to go to Boston?"

"Far as I know." Folding his hands on top of his head, Vinnie tipped back in his chair so the front two legs left the floor as he stared at Edna. "Classes are over, so when she lost her job, she decided to go home a couple of days early."

"What time was she at the shelter?" Edna not only wanted to know if Bethany might have seen Mary, but she also thought the information would be of interest to Charlie. Bethany seemed to have been in the vicinity at the pertinent time yesterday.

Vinnie shrugged again, raising his elbows as well as his shoulders with the motion. "Must've been around four. Maybe a little before, maybe a little after. I dunno. She borrowed the bike from my uncle. He and I were helping get ready for supper customers at the Kitchen when she brought it back. That's when she asked if I'd take her to the train station."

"What did Laurel say to her?" Edna was thinking fast. Charlie should know about this. Maybe Bethany was the last one to see Laurel alive. Maybe they'd quarreled. The idea dissolved with Vinnie's next words.

"She didn't talk to Laurel. Didn't see her at all."

Edna raised her eyebrows. "How do you know?"

"She told me. Said the Perrys' car was in the driveway. She wanted to see Laurel alone. Didn't want to make a scene with others around, I guess."

"The Perrys' car?" Edna thought for a few seconds before asking, "Their car or the van?"

He shook his head. "I don't remember. She might have said 'van'."

Edna felt exasperated. She needed to speak with Bethany herself, or Charlie needed to. At the moment though, Vinnie would have to do. "She biked all that way and then didn't go inside or talk to anyone? What *did* she do?"

He dropped his hands from his head and leaned forward, bringing the chair's front legs back to the floor with a thud. "She said she rode around the block a couple of times, but she was getting cold, so she decided she wouldn't wait around any longer. She just headed back to town." He was speaking brusquely now, as if he were tired of the conversation or annoyed at Edna's tone.

In turn, Edna speculated. Had Bethany told Vinnie the truth, or had she, in fact, gone into the house? Had she another reason for leaving town so suddenly last night? Edna didn't voice these thoughts to the young man sitting across the table. Instead, she asked without much hope of a positive answer, "Did she say whether or not she saw Mary at the shelter?"

He picked up his mug and took a drink, grimaced and shook his head at the coffee. "Cold," he complained.

Edna wondered if he were trying to stall or change the subject. "Do you know? Did she mention Mary at all?"

He shook his head again, this time at Edna. "She

didn't, but if Mary had been there, Bethany would have felt better about going inside. She likes Mary, says she's a good friend." He put his hands on the table, hesitating a second before pushing himself up. Obviously, he'd had enough of Edna's questions.

Before she could think of anything else to ask him, Gran came out of the kitchen, speaking as she burst through the double doors. "Sorry to keep you waiting, Edna, but Priscilla wanted to start the soup. She doesn't expect many customers today, what with the weather and all, so we made just the tomato bisque. Said between Vinnie here and his uncle, they can handle anyone who comes by. She's decided to close early, too, so she can get to her Christmas party, so she said she won't need me to lock up tonight."

"How you doin', Gran?" Vinnie stood and picked up both his and Edna's mugs, stacked them with his dishes and pushed his chair up to the table.

"Fine, Vinnie. How's life treating you these days? All ready for Christmas?" She returned the greeting and looked around and out toward the street. Not waiting for answers to her questions, she asked another. "Where's your uncle today?"

"Dunno. Thought he'd be here by now. Might have slid into a snow bank. The tires on that truck of his are as bald as a bowling ball. I'm gonna go check on him as soon as I wash up these dishes. I've been trying to get Uncle Codfish to get rid of that old hunk of metal. The rusty old thing is on its last legs, but he keeps telling me he is too, so they get along just fine."

Gran laughed at Vinnie's good-natured grin, as Edna finally realized the connection. "Codfish?" She didn't believe there could be two men in town with the same nickname. "Codfish McKale is your uncle?"

"Great-uncle, actually," Vinnie said with a look of pride. "Best fisherman in these parts until arthritis got too much for him."

"I hope you're wrong about him being stuck in a snow drift," Gran said. "When you see him, tell him I won't be working tonight, will you?" Again, without waiting for an answer, she turned to Edna. "Ready to go?"

Driving home, Edna was quiet, thinking about Mary. Where could she be? Had she seen Bethany yesterday afternoon? Expanding on the thought, Edna's heart skipped a beat. What if Mary had seen Bethany push Laurel down the stairs? Instantly, Edna shook off the idea of Mary covering up a crime, but before she could gather her thoughts again, Gran's voice distracted her. They had reached their neighborhood.

"Will you come in and let me make lunch for you? It's the least I can do for your taking the time to chauffeur me around this morning."

About to answer as they reached Mary's property, Edna's attention was diverted to a pickup plowing out the driveway. When she noticed the sign "Honeydew Home Repairs" on the driver's door and noticed who was behind the wheel, she waved to Kevin. Having liked Tom's nephew, her resolve to never again give her business to Norm Wilkins' company weakened, particularly when, driving on, she saw that her own driveway was untouched. Last night's snowfall hadn't been as heavy as she'd feared, but although the current snow was light and gentle, it had already laid another inch or two on top of the existing six.

She was about to reply to Gran's invitation when a huge, box-shaped vehicle appeared around the corner, heading straight toward the Kia, halfway into Edna's lane on the narrow road. Curiously, the driver turned the wiper speed up a notch and sprayed washer fluid across the windshield. Although somewhat erratic, fortunately, the oncoming behemoth was moving slowly. Closing in on Gran's driveway, Edna aimed the Kia for the foot of the macadam and, stepping on the gas, swerved in off the road with less than a car length to spare as the giant vehicle lumbered by. The Kia's engine had stalled, so Edna sat for a minute, waiting for her heart rate to slow. In the fleeting seconds of avoiding a collision and because of the other vehicle's frosty wet windshield, Edna had seen only a shadowy silhouette of the driver.

She took several deep breaths to calm her nerves before turning to Gran. "Do you recognize that car?"

"Never seen it before. Have you?"

Edna shook her head and, restarting the engine, drove up the slope to park in front of the garage. She accepted Gran's invitation to lunch and forced her thoughts to matters other than automobile accidents. She spoke to herself as much as to Gran when she said, "If Mary called Kevin to clear her driveway, she might be home. I'll phone her and maybe she can ask him to plow my drive while we have lunch."

Rummaging in her tote bag for the cell phone, she suddenly remembered connecting it to the charger on her desk. She'd had so much on her mind when she left the house that morning, she hadn't grabbed the mobile. "I'll also need to use your phone, Gran," she said, feeling at once deflated and tired.

Obviously pleased to have company, Gran led the way across the back deck to the kitchen door and, seating Edna at the white table, handed her a cordless receiver before tying an apron around her stout waist. "You go ahead and make your calls while I rustle up something to eat."

Edna first tried Mary's home phone. A thought nagged at the back of her mind as the message machine picked up. Fighting back frustration, she left an "urgent" message for Mary to call her before she then dialed Mary's cell number. Once again, Edna heard the recording. "Leave a message," was all Mary said to whomever reached her voice mailbox.

Worry was turning into anger and annoyance by the time Edna dialed her own home number to check the answering machine. After punching in the retrieval code and listening to two new messages, thoughts of Mary vanished.

The first call had been from Charlie. "I have news. Call me."

The second was from her daughter. "Mother, it's me. Diane. If you're there, please pick up." After a short pause during which her daughter apparently realized that Edna was not purposely ignoring her, Diane went on. "I'm at the hospital with Father. Call me back as soon as you get this message."

Chapter 12

Alarmed by the urgency in Diane's voice, Edna phoned her daughter first. "What's going on?" she asked as soon as Diane picked up the call. "Why are you at the hospital?"

"First, let me say that Father is okay. He'll be fine."

Diane's habit of never getting directly to the point did nothing to assuage Edna's fright, so she spoke more sharply than she'd intended. "What happened?"

"He fell."

Edna waited several seconds for some further explanation before finally taking a deep breath to control her rising agitation. How exasperating was this daughter of Albert's. Thinking of the old family joke whereby they swapped parentage, depending on said child's behavior, made her relax slightly and allowed her to ask with relative calm. "How did he fall?"

"He was testing out his new brace. It's adjustable as to the degree he can bend his knee."

"Yes. He explained that to me." Edna waited a few seconds, but when Diane didn't continue, she said, "Did he fall on the damaged knee?"

"No, Mother, and he probably would have been okay falling on the carpeted floor, but he banged his head on the coffee table." Diane paused, but hurried on before Edna had a chance to speak again. "Actually, the doctors don't know if the brace was at fault or if Father fainted. Whatever the cause, he was groggy and couldn't get up. We were alone in the house and I wasn't able to lift him. I thought he needed to be checked for concussion." Diane was babbling by this point, but whether to get the story out or to absolve herself of guilt, Edna didn't know. "I called nine-one-one," Diane finally faltered.

Now Edna understood. If he thought he hadn't hurt himself seriously, Albert probably would have been embarrassed to arrive at the hospital in an ambulance--and particularly, he would not enjoy being fussed over by people he had worked with professionally for years. She didn't voice these thoughts, but asked instead, "You said he was fine, so why are you still at the hospital?"

"In case his fall was caused by low blood pressure or there's a chance something might be going on with his heart, the doctor wants an echocardiogram before he releases Father."

"Does Albert want to see me? Do you need my help?"

"No, Mother, that's okay. It's snowing again and the roads are getting slick. I don't want to have to worry about you, too. I'll let you know as soon as I hear from the doctor."

Edna was beginning to realize that Diane had really only wanted to talk and be reassured that she had done the right thing. "I'm relieved to know you're taking such good care of your father. Thank you, dear."

Diane sounded more relaxed and confident when she spoke. "You're welcome, Mother. I've been enjoying his company, and Buddy absolutely adores having his grandfather to himself."

"Is Albert nearby? May I speak with him?"

"They took him down for tests a few minutes before you phoned. I'll have him call when they're through with him."

Hanging up shortly thereafter, Edna took several deep breaths, allowing her nerves to settle and her adrenaline to dissolve. Reassured that Albert wasn't badly hurt, she turned her mind to the second call of that morning.

"Not a word," Charlie replied to Edna's question as to whether or not he'd heard from Mary. "The patrolman I sent over to her house said the place felt empty. You can usually tell if someone is home and just not answering the door. He didn't even hear Hank bark."

"Did he go around to the kitchen door?"

"Yep. Knocked on both front and back doors. Rang the bell. Walked around the house and looked in windows. He knows to look for Ink Spot in the window beside the back door, but he heard and saw nothing."

"Do you want to go inside? I have a key to her house."

Charlie snorted. "He could have gone in. My guy spotted the fake rock she uses to hide a house key. Saw it right off. She shouldn't keep it so close to the door."

"It's not her key in the rock." Edna couldn't keep the self-satisfaction from her voice.

She nearly laughed aloud at the silence that followed her announcement. Having been threatened by a man who had snuck into her house earlier that year, Edna had come up with a plan to thwart any future intruders. Her house key was kept in an artificial rock by Mary's back door while Mary's key was in the bottom of a plastic green frog in the Davies' garden. Of course, someone could probably find either key fairly quickly, but it wouldn't open any door in the nearest house.

"Pretty clever," Charlie said when she explained, "but even if we had access to a spare key, we can't go into someone's home without permission or a warrant." From Charlie's tone, he might as well have added, "you should know that by now."

Edna remembered the truck she'd seen as they'd driven into the neighborhood. "Kevin Lockhorn was plowing Mary's driveway. She must have called him, don't you think?"

"I didn't know he was out there," Charlie said. "She usually hires the Benton brothers down the street. Teenagers. She has a standing agreement with them, so even if she isn't home, they'd shovel and check back later to get paid." After another brief pause during which Edna figured he was probably making a note, he said, "I'll give Kevin a call and find out if he heard from her."

Edna thought for a minute. "He might not have. It's possible he could be plowing her out as a favor. Mary has been a family friend since her high school years." Edna didn't know Kevin's personal phone number, so she couldn't call him directly. She shuddered at the idea of phoning Honeydew Home

Repairs and having to ask Norm to speak to Kevin. To Charlie, she said, "If you talk to Kevin, let me know what he says, will you? I'd like to know that *someone* has heard from Mary."

She went on to tell him what she'd learned from Vinnie and the possible timing of Bethany's bike ride to and from the CATS shelter. She asked the detective what he thought of the young woman deciding to leave so quickly for Boston, but he seemed to agree with Vinnie that there had been no reason for her to hang around if she wasn't working or going to class.

"Good to know where to find her, though," he said. "I'll see if my contact in Boston can go talk to our young lady."

"Will you let me know what she says?"

"Sure thing, Edna. Soon as I hear myself. Anything else?"

She hesitated only a second or two. "As a matter of fact, there is. Do you think I could hire those teenagers to plow my driveway?"

"You bet. They're always on the lookout for odd jobs. I need to call them and find out if they might have heard from Mary, so I'll let them know you need their services. If you haven't been shoveled out within the next couple of hours, call me back."

Before he could hang up, she asked about the message he'd left. "What's the news you called about this morning, if it wasn't that you'd heard from Mary?"

"I got a preliminary back on Laurel Taylor from the medical examiner. Her neck was broken when she fell down the stairs. The M.E. found signs of a struggle, so that leaves out accidental death. She had bruises on her upper arms where someone grabbed her. Looks like someone slapped her hard on the side of her face, too. According to the report, there's a pretty clear handprint. The lab work won't be back on poison in her system for a while yet, but it's possible someone either held her by the arms and pushed her backwards or the slap might have caused her to step backwards and fall. The autopsy should be able to tell us which injury happened first."

"Oh, my." Edna was stunned by the thought of Laurel being attacked or pushed to her death.

"That's not all," he went on. "Report says she had older injuries. Broken forearm, maybe as old as two or three years. Couple of broken ribs, older than the arm fracture. Her collar bone has been broken, too, at some point. She's been beaten more than once as an adult. None are from childhood."

"A battered wife?" Edna's stomach clenched at the thought.

"All the signs point to it, but we won't know for sure until we find her next of kin, or someone who knew her before she moved to town. We might be able to get hospital records once we find out where she came from. I'm working on that, but I haven't turned up anything so far. I'm on my way back to the house now to look for her papers, see if I can find an address book or something."

By the time Edna finished speaking with Charlie, Gran had lunch ready and placed bowls of chicken soup on the table. She went back to the counter for a basket of hot, cheesy buttermilk biscuits before sitting down opposite Edna. As the aroma of the bullion rose from the steaming dish, Edna realized how hungry she was.

Breaking open one of the biscuits, Gran said, "I couldn't help but overhear your conversation. Did I hear you say Laurel Taylor was a battered wife? Is that who you were talking about?"

"Yes." Edna raised her spoon toward her mouth. She didn't want to discuss something so unpleasant during lunch. She also wanted time to absorb the news herself. "Everything looks and smells so good. Thank you for lunch."

Gran took the hint. The women ate in silence for several minutes before she put aside her spoon to select another biscuit from the basket. "What did Charlie say about Mary? Has he heard from her?"

Having finished only half her meal, Edna's appetite vanished with the question. "No, he hasn't. So far, the only thing we know is that one of the neighbors saw her rushing away from CATS late yesterday afternoon. Vinnie's friend may or may not have seen Mary at the shelter, but she's gone home to Boston for the holidays." Unable to stop a rising fear, Edna looked across the table at her hostess. "I'm really getting worried about Mary. I've got to find her and make sure she's okay. She's never disappeared like this before."

With a vigorous nod of her head, Gran slapped the table on either side of her soup bowl, palms down. "What can I do to help?"

Turning to look out the window at the deck, Edna noticed the snow hadn't let up. "I don't want to be out in this weather longer than necessary, so we should have a plan." She pushed aside her half-empty soup bowl and picked up the tote bag she'd set on the chair beside her. Rummaging inside, she pulled out a small notepad and a pencil.

"You'll probably need a bigger sheet of paper than that," Gran said, her tone edged with excitement as she rose and gathered up the lunch dishes. After depositing them in the kitchen sink, she grabbed the electric kettle and filled it from the faucet. "Tea will help, and I'll get some paper from Carol's computer room. She keeps a stack of it next to her printer." Minutes later, she returned with a thin sheaf of letter-sized paper and a plastic cup full of pens, pencils and markers which she plunked down on the table as she removed the bread basket. At that moment, the kettle began to whistle. Gran turned to make the tea while Edna selected a sheet of paper.

"I think we should stop at Mary's house first. I don't know what we'll find, but we'll look for anything out of the ordinary." As she spoke, Edna began her list.

"Where are her pets?" Gran asked. She poured boiling water into a teapot, covered it with a cozy and opened an overhead cupboard that held an array of mugs.

"Good question." Edna thought for a minute before she brightened. "Why don't we go pick up your kitten at Perry's Clinic. At the same time, we can check with Doctor Jake and Roselyn. If Hank and Spot aren't with Mary, she'd probably have left them at the clinic. At any rate, they might at least have heard from her."

Gran set the teapot and mugs in the middle of the table and went back to the counter for a plate of brownies. "We need chocolate to go with our tea. Helps us think better," she said with a grin. She was obviously pleased that Edna had asked for her help. "How nice of you to remember about my kitten." She sat as Edna continued to make notes. "You said someone saw Mary at the shelter yesterday afternoon. Shall we go there, too? Maybe we can talk to some of the neighbors."

"That was next on my list," Edna agreed, scribbling rapidly. "Charlie spoke to at least one person who said she saw Bethany. Maybe that person can tell us if she saw Mary at the same time. I'd like to go back to Krispin's Kitchen and talk to Vinnie. He might remember something else they talked about when he drove Bethany to the train station. At the very least, he should have her phone number. Charlie's sending someone to talk to her, but I want to speak with her, too."

Thoughts of the young woman in Boston made Edna think of her youngest daughter at that moment. If Starling weren't visiting her brother in Colorado, she might have been called upon to visit the Marco family and question Bethany herself. Edna sighed, missing her daughter particularly at that moment. She'd have liked to talk things over with her youngest child who had shared more than one mishap with her.

Having jotted down the obvious first steps, she accepted the mug Gran held out and took a cautious sip of the hot liquid. After a moment's thought, she said, "I'd like to find the woman with the blue car.

I'm not certain how she fits into the picture, but I got the impression she wasn't one of Laurel's volunteers … or one of Laurel's admirers," Edna added, remembering the woman who had stormed out of CATS and nearly knocked her down the previous morning.

"How are we to do that, find someone based on the color of a car?" Gran picked up a brownie and nibbled a corner.

"I don't know." Edna gave a rueful smile. "We could use Mary's expertise with this," she said dryly. "I'll add the blue-car woman to our list, and we can figure out how to go about finding her after we've investigated these other avenues." Dutifully, she wrote down *Woman with blue car, license ending 32*. Immediately, she thought of something else and wrote *Did Mary contact Kevin to plow her driveway?*

"In case Charlie is too busy to contact him beforehand, I'd like to find a personal phone number for Kevin Lockhorn, but I'm not certain how to do that either. He's new in town, so wouldn't be listed. He's probably got only a cell, at any rate," Edna spoke aloud, more to herself than to Gran. "And I'd like to talk to any of Laurel's volunteers we can find. I'm grabbing at straws, but it's possible that Mary might have contacted one of them. Charlie's going over to look for Laurel's papers. I might be able to get a list of the volunteers from him."

"Speaking of volunteering," Gran said, "doesn't Mary do some work at the local hospital? Do you suppose she might have been in touch with someone there?"

"Gran, you're a genius," Edna said, adding the South County Hospital to her list. "She hates to miss visiting the patients with the book cart. Certainly, she'd call to let them know if she wasn't going to show up for her shift." Sitting back in the chair, Edna pushed her list to the middle of the table where Gran could see it, realizing as she did so that she had just created another to-do list.

*And with all I have to do in the next two days-- Christmas cards, housecleaning, grocery shopping, cooking* ... She was immediately ashamed of herself. Everything else could wait. Finding Mary was the most important task she had right now.

"Oh, my," said Gran, as if reading Edna's next thought, "where do we begin?"

Chapter 13

Once decided on a plan and having straightened up the kitchen, Edna and Gran set out for Mary's house. First, Edna had to find the green plastic frog in the herb garden at her own house to retrieve her neighbor's key. By now, accumulation was nearing eight inches and the snow was still falling, quietly and gently but persistently. She would have to burrow to find a four-inch-tall frog.

She carefully backed down Gran's slippery driveway, skidding at the bottom as she gave the Kia more gas to get over a mound of snow left by the road plows while the women had been having lunch. She'd expected to park alongside the road and trudge the hundred yards to her house, but found to her delight that someone had plowed her driveway. There didn't seem to have been enough time since she'd spoken to Charlie for the teenagers to have done the job, so she guessed the Good Samaritan had been Kevin, having recently seen him plowing Mary's driveway. She was silently blessing him until she got around the sleigh and reindeer in the middle of her circular drive. He had pushed the snow hard up against the front and rear bumpers of her car. *What strange behavior*, she thought with a sudden surge of doubt as to the man's mental stability. *Why would he do such a thing?*

"Look what someone's done," Gran exclaimed, giving voice to Edna's thoughts.

"Kevin Lockhorn, most likely." Edna frowned, studying the packed snow as she eased the Kia past her Buick sedan and pulled up in front of it.

"The man I met at your party last night?" Gran's disbelief was evident. "He seemed so nice, I wouldn't have thought he'd do something like this."

"There must be an explanation," Edna said, still unable to understand the bizarre behavior. Had Kevin really done this or had someone else? He was the only one she'd seen plowing snow in the neighborhood. Was it his idea of a joke?

Sitting for a minute to ponder the situation, Edna decided she'd take time to get her cell phone from the house and call Charlie before searching for the frog containing Mary's key. Since he was going to call Kevin to ask if he'd heard from Mary, Charlie might also be able to find out why Kevin would have blocked her car. When she first met him, she'd marveled at how much he looked like his uncle and, most likely because of that resemblance, she'd assumed he had a personality to match. Tom Greene never would have behaved in the manner just displayed by his nephew. Now, she wondered if Kevin might be more like his cousin. Norm Wilkins was as malicious and cruel as Tom had been thoughtful and kind.

She pushed the suppositions firmly from her mind. This was no time to sit and speculate. She'd ask Charlie to send the Benton brothers over to dig out her car. If they'd already been by and seen that the entrance at the road had been cleared, they wouldn't have come up to the house. Not only the large oak tree but also the Christmas sleigh and reindeer in the middle of the circle would have blocked the boys' view. Besides getting rid of the snow packed around her vehicle, the Bentons could shovel the stoop at the front door and the brick path around to the back.

"Wait here, Gran. I won't be long." Edna left the motor running to continue warming the car. Stepping out, she noticed footsteps in the snow leading around the side of the house. Oddly, the left boot heel looked as if a piece of the inside edge had been sliced off. She was grateful for someone having tramped down the snow, probably Kevin, but disturbed as to what he'd been doing. He hadn't bothered to shovel the walk, so why had he come this way?

Following the footsteps to the back door, she was relieved when she entered the mudroom to find Benjamin in his bed. He yawned and blinked at her, apparently having been awakened from an afternoon nap. If anyone had been in the house, Benjamin would not be acting so casual. Giving his ears a rub, she told him to go back to sleep and hurried through the kitchen to her small office off the front hallway.

When Charlie didn't pick up her call, she wasn't concerned. If he was busy, he generally checked to see who was calling and, if he decided it had nothing to do with work, let it ring through to voice messaging. She left a brief request for him to call the Bentons and to call her back when he had the time, preferably before he spoke with Kevin. Just as well. Explaining about her blocked car and the footprints would take time, and Gran was waiting in the Kia. Having left her message, she slipped the phone into her coat pocket and went out to scuff around in the snow for a four-inch high, green plastic frog.

Once they arrived at Mary's back door, Gran insisted on accompanying Edna into the house. "I'm not letting you go in alone," she announced, unbuckling her seat belt.

As had become her habit, Edna used the back door which opened into the hall off the kitchen. Opposite the door, a set of stairs led to the second floor. The house was cold and silent. *Not cold enough for the pipes to burst*, Edna thought with relief. It felt as though the heat were on, but not set too high, the way it would be left if Mary planned to be away for a while. Was that a good sign or not, Edna wondered and thought about the party to be held here in two days' time.

"What a lovely old house." Gran's voice brought Edna out of her musings. The older woman had moved past Edna and gone into the kitchen where she stood in the archway to the dining room. She was looking through to a bank of tall windows that allowed a panoramic view of the yard, stone walls and woods at the back of the house.

"I never saw these rooms in their original state, so I can only imagine how gloomy they were. About three years ago, at a friend's suggestion, Mary had the wall between the two rooms replaced with the archway and added those big windows. It *is* nice, isn't it," Edna said.

The sides of the archway consisted of narrow open shelves which could be reached from either side. Mary's answering machine, its red message light blinking steadily, stood on one of the shelves. Edna stopped to investigate as Gran, apparently enthralled with the view to the outside, moved to the windows at the end of the dining room.

Mesmerized by the blinking red light on the machine, Edna was trying to decide whether or not to listen to the calls when the thought that had been nagging at the back of her mind finally crystalized. *Mary was in this house after Charlie phoned me last night. He said he hadn't left a message because the machine hadn't been on.*

She didn't want to intrude on Mary's privacy, but maybe Mary herself had recorded something. Any straight-thinking person would have called Edna directly, but it would be just like Mary to leave a message on her own machine and expect Edna to find it. Still, she hesitated, staring at the blinking light, slowly rubbing her hand up and down her thigh. Finally making up her mind, she reached out and was about to push the "play back" button when Gran's voice brought her up with a start.

"Somebody's been walking around out here."

Responding to the urgency in Gran's tone, Edna hurried through to where she stood pointing to footprints in the snow.

Remembering Charlie's conversation, Edna thought at first the prints might have been made by the patrolman who had come to see if Mary was home. "These tracks can't be from the police officer," she said, dismissing the idea instantly. "He was here before the heavy snowfall."

"These are fresh prints," Gran agreed, leaning with her head almost touching the glass as she looked down at tracks beneath the window. "There's a light dusting of snow in them, so I'd say he was here within the last hour. Otherwise, the prints would either be completely covered up or barely visible." She turned to look up at Edna. "How am I doing as a detective?" she asked with a mischievous grin.

Edna couldn't help but smile back before turning serious. Whoever it had been--and the prints looked to be those of a man or a large woman--they had walked close to the house after having gone to investigate the outbuilding nestled in the trees off to the left as the women stared out over the scene. Originally, the outbuilding had been a buggy barn and now was where Mary garaged her Jeep when she wanted it under cover.

"You're right," Edna said, thinking of the footprints leading to her own back door. She noticed the distinctive tread, as if a piece of the left heel had been cut away. She was certain the same person had walked around both houses. "The snow hasn't had a chance to obliterate them. I'm thinking that Kevin probably took a walk around the place when he finished plowing." *But why*, she wondered silently.

"You don't think it was Mary? Should we go look in that shed?"

Edna slowly shook her head, considering as she spoke. "The tracks are too big. Mary is tall, but her feet are narrow. And I don't think anyone is in the buggy barn. The tracks go in, but then come out again and up to the house. I'm fairly certain it was Kevin. I think he did the same at my place when he was there to plow the driveway, but he only went to my back door. Here, it looks like he made a circuit of the house in order to look in the windows."

"Do you think he was trying to find a way in?"

Gran's question made Edna's heart skip a beat. Was he hiding somewhere in the house or had someone else been here after Kevin left? She calmed somewhat when she thought of the empty driveway. In this sparsely-settled neighborhood and in this weather, the trespasser would certainly have driven in, and she would have noticed more tire tracks. No vehicles had been parked anywhere nearby that she had seen. She thought briefly of Charlie's mystery bicyclist and dismissed that thought, too. However hardy that soul was, nobody would be riding a bike on these snow-packed and icy roads.

When she'd parked in front of Mary's house a few minutes ago, she'd noticed fresh tire tracks, almost certainly left by Kevin's truck. Of course, she thought, he must have been the one nosing around the property, but why? It didn't make sense when he would be welcomed inside by either Mary or by Edna herself. Why skulk around when nobody was home?

At that moment, she wanted to leave as quickly as possible, but not before she'd investigated the place. Turning abruptly, she said, "I'll just make a quick check of the upstairs rooms. Then, let's get out of here."

"I'm coming with you," Gran said, sounding as spooked as Edna felt.

With her elderly companion following close behind, Edna went through to the foyer and mounted the wide, curving front stairs to make a quick tour of the upper two floors. Most of the rooms were closed off, so she merely stuck her head in each door, murmuring aloud what she could remember Mary telling her the year before when Edna had spent a night in the old house. With Edna muttering such explanations as "Mrs. Osbourne's room" and "Mary's old nursery," the two women hurried through the dark hallways.

The two rooms Edna actually entered, Mary's bedroom and its adjacent sitting room, were on the second floor. The furniture was highly polished and the canopied bed neatly made. At the foot of the quilt-covered bed lay a squarely folded stadium blanket. For Spot, Edna guessed. On the floor beside the four-poster was a large, red plaid dog's bed.

In the sitting room, two overstuffed chairs framed a small fireplace. A twenty-five inch flat-screen television stood on a sturdy mahogany table and, on either side of the door leading out to the hallway, the walls consisted of built-in shelves, stuffed to overflowing with books and magazines. A round braided rug covered the parquet floor and an end table with a reading lamp sat next to a floral-patterned settee. Almost unconsciously, Edna noticed again that the two rooms were on the north side of the house, with a fine view of her own house and backyard patio.

A tour of the top floor, half of which had once been Mary's playroom and the other half attic space, led them around to the back stairs. Other than an occasional, softly spoken remark like "Lovely" or "How nice" over an antique table or Tiffany lampshade, Gran had been silent during their investigations. Edna had seen nothing out of the ordinary and no sign of where Mary might have gone. She was certain her neighbor had been in the house the previous night, and she was just as certain Mary hadn't slept there. So where was she? And where were Hank and Spot?

These thoughts spun in Edna's head as the two women reached and descended the back stairs. Edna ushered Gran out of the house and carefully locked the door behind them. As she thought again of the animals, she relaxed slightly. Certainly their absence was a good sign. If Mary had been at the house to adjust the heat and collect her pets, she wasn't hurt, nor was she being held against her will.

"Do you think we should look in that old barn?" Gran asked again. Apparently, there was something about the building that was calling to her.

Edna hesitated, not wanting to trudge through more snow, but her better sense took over. Gran was correct to suggest a thorough search, and at once, Edna had to know for certain if Mary's Jeep were there. If she had come home last night before the storm, she might have garaged the vehicle and gone off with someone else. So, leaving Gran in the

Kia again with the motor running, Edna trekked to the buggy barn to find it empty. No Jeep and no sign of Mary.

On the road again, Edna thought they should stop at Krispin's Kitchen before heading for CATS. She wanted to speak to Vinnie and get a phone number for Bethany. Charlie was sending someone to talk to the young woman, but if Edna didn't hear back by this evening, she intended to phone Bethany herself. When they arrived at the restaurant, it was to find Codfish McKale, but not his nephew. The old man was busy sweeping the floor around the tables, a once-white bib apron tied over his flannel plaid shirt and worn blue jeans. As the two women entered, Codfish raised his head from his task with an expression of annoyance that lunch time was over and the restaurant door should have been locked, but at the sight of Gran, his wizened face broke into such a look of joy, Edna thought immediately of a bud opening to full flower.

"Watcha doin' here?" he asked, leaning on the broom handle and not taking his eyes off Edna's companion for a second. He was grinning broadly and when Edna turned to look at Gran, the old woman had the same expression on her face.

*Ahhh, true love*, Edna thought, smiling to herself as she looked from man to woman.

The frozen tableau was shattered by a middle-aged woman who burst through the swinging doors from the kitchen. "Sorry, we're closing for the day," she said before recognition dawned as she spotted Gran. "Oh, it's you, Gran. I thought I sent you home. What are you doing out in this weather?"

"Hi, Priscilla. I don't think you had a chance this morning to meet my friend and neighbor, Edna Davies." Turning to Edna, Gran said, "This is Priscilla Powell." At once, she extended a palm to Codfish, "And do you know Codfish McKale?"

The two restaurant employees nodded to Edna who acknowledged their greetings with a small wave of her hand and a "Nice to meet you."

Gran turned to Codfish. "Edna wants to talk to Vinnie. Is he still around?"

"Nope." Codfish shook his head. "Left an hour ago."

"Do you know where we can find him?" Edna tried to keep the disappointment out of her voice. Nothing was going right. Whatever she tried seemed to bring her no closer to finding Mary, and now her mind kept turning back to Kevin Lockhorn's odd behavior. She was finding it hard to stay focused. Concentrating on why she'd come back to the diner, she said to Codfish, "Do you have a number where I can reach your nephew?"

"Yup, sure do. It's at home by my phone," the old man said. "That's the only place I call him from. Haven't the need, otherwise. Don't carry one of those tiny, tinny, fancy phones. Can't hear a blame thing on 'em."

"I have his number," Priscilla spoke up, "but it's in my purse out in the trunk of my car." When she saw the quizzical look on Edna's face, she explained. "I've already loaded everything in my car. I only came back in to tell Codfish to quit working and lock up. With this storm and all, we won't be open for supper tonight."

When Priscilla didn't volunteer to go out and get her purse, Edna said, "If I give you my phone number, will you call me with his number as soon as you can?" She dug a pen out of her bag and, going to the counter, quickly wrote down both her cell and home phone numbers on a paper napkin. Handing it to Priscilla, she said, "It's important that I reach him."

The snow had stopped falling by the time Edna and Gran were back in the Kia and heading for Laurel Taylor's house, but, looking at the sky, Edna could tell the storm was by no means over.

"Do you think Priscilla will call me?" Edna asked Gran.

"I'm sure she will, but if you don't hear from her, let me know and I'll phone her. Priscilla's mother and I are old childhood friends, you know."

Gran talked on, but Edna was so intent on driving that she was conscious only that the older woman was talking about someone named Faye and would occasionally mention Codfish. Fortunately, there weren't many cars on the road, but the few who were had Edna's full attention. Finally arriving at the cat shelter, she noticed Charlie Rogers' car in the driveway and pulled in behind his vehicle.

"What brings you out here?" Charlie looked surprised and not too pleased to see the women standing on the porch when he opened the door to their knock.

"Nice to see you, too, Charlie," Edna said, smiling in an attempt to disarm him. "I was hoping to get a list of Laurel's volunteers. I thought I'd contact them to see if anyone has heard from Mary," she added when he didn't return the smile and didn't move aside to let them enter the house.

"I'd like to hear from her myself," he said, rubbing a hand through his hair. "Look, Edna, you've been helpful in the past, but I'm afraid you're getting in the way this time. I'm the one who needs to find Mary, not you. She's probably the last person to have seen the victim alive and, as such, she's a valuable witness for my investigation."

Edna felt her eyes widen. "Except for the murderer, you mean. The murderer would have been the last to see the victim alive. You're not thinking that Mary had anything to do with Laurel's death, are you?"

"No," Charlie said with a snort, brushing aside the idea. "But she was seen driving off at a pretty fast clip. Now she's nowhere to be found and she doesn't answer her phones." With those words, he pulled his own mobile from the holster on his belt and punched in some numbers.

As she watched him put the phone to his ear, Edna thought she heard a distant, muffled ringing. She turned and cocked her head, trying to figure out where the noise was coming from. Slowly, she walked down the stairs and started wading through calf-high snow when the sound stopped. She turned to see Charlie putting the phone back into its holder.

"Charlie, did you just try to call Mary?"

"Yes. Why?"

"Dial her number again, will you?"

With a frown and a shrug and watching Edna intently, he complied.

"What is it?" Gran asked from the porch steps.

Not answering, Edna cocked her head and turned again toward Charlie's car in the driveway as the ringing tone sounded again. "Don't hang up unless voice mail kicks in," she called over her shoulder as she moved as quickly as the snow would allow. When the ringing stopped, she looked back at Charlie to see that he was redialing. Almost at once, the ringing started up once more. As she bent and brushed away the snow beside the driveway, the ringing grew louder. With a final swipe of her hand, she hit something and saw the stainless steel phone shoot up with the handful of snow she'd raised.

It was ringing and it was Mary's.

## Chapter 14

"That explains why she hasn't answered her mobile." Charlie trudged through the snow to reach Edna's side. "I'll take that," he said, reaching for the ice-encrusted phone.

Handing it over, she said, "It may explain her not answering this particular phone, but it doesn't explain why she hasn't been home or called us from somewhere else."

"Do you think she might have been kidnapped?" Gran asked, her eyes wide over the recent discovery.

Astonished by the idea, Edna nearly laughed at its absurdity. But was the notion so far-fetched? What would cause Mary to leave home and not contact her friends? Before Edna could voice her own questions, Charlie spoke.

"Hold on. Let's not jump to conclusions." He put a gentling hand on Gran's shoulder and looked from her to Edna. "Mary was seen driving away from here yesterday afternoon. Alone. Nobody else was in the car. Finding her phone here in the snow, we might assume that, at one point, she stepped out of her car. On the other hand, we don't know if she went into the house or stood here talking to someone or threw her phone out the window ..." He paused, as if considering why Mary might have thrown the phone or what else she might have been doing for her mobile to be found lying next to the driveway. Instead of making further assumptions, he smiled at Edna. "You know Mary and how she loves to watch people, how she tries to hide in plain sight. It's one reason she wears those camo clothes. She's probably off on one of her campaigns. I'll bet she doesn't even know she's lost her phone, but as soon as she discovers it's missing, she'll be calling you to see if she left it at your house."

Knowing he was trying to allay her fears, Edna couldn't help but smile back at him as she thought of some of the quirky things Mary had done, but she sobered quickly. "I can't think she'd be playing games for this long, particularly with her big holiday party only two days away, Charlie. What if she's had an accident? Have you contacted the hospitals?"

He sighed and shook his head, rubbing a hand across his chin in frustration. "I've been concentrating on the murder site, not on Mary, but I want to find her even more than you. As I said before, she's probably the last person to see the victim alive. So far, all I've been doing is dialing her phone periodically. Until now, I didn't know the darn cell was just lying here under the snow."

"Are you officially off vacation and back on duty?" Edna asked.

"Yes, but assigned only to this case. We're short-handed and with the storm, road accidents, and emergency calls, not to mention the flu that's going around, I'm having to beg for what little assistance I can get. Despite the M.E.'s report, the chief still isn't totally convinced Laurel's death wasn't just an unfortunate accident--woman tripping or fainting and falling down stairs. He says the fall could have caused the bruises on her arms and face. Personally, I think he's trying to justify not assigning anyone else to help me, but it wouldn't be a wise career move to challenge him." Charlie's lips turned up at the corners as if to let the women know he was making light of the situation, but his eyes remained sad and serious.

Edna felt as exasperated as Charlie sounded. "What should we do about Mary, then? How do we find her?"

He glanced from Edna to Gran and back. "I know you're worried about her. I am too. But look, everyone in the department knows her, at least by sight, and most would recognize her Jeep. We're all keeping an eye out, and I've asked the dispatcher to let me know if any accidents come in involving a ragtop. So far, I've heard nothing, so she's probably fine." This time his smile did reach his eyes when he said, "You know Mary. She can take care of herself." He extended an arm, palm up, toward their car. "Why don't you go home and get out of this cold. I promise to call as soon as I hear anything."

Ignoring his suggestion for the moment, Edna stood her ground and repeated her earlier question. "What about the hospitals? Have you called to see if she's been admitted to the South County? They might not give me information about a patient, but they'd confide in a police officer, wouldn't they?"

At this, Gran spoke up. "If Mary's supervisor is also a volunteer, she might not have to abide by confidentiality rules. Talking to her is on our list. Maybe we can swing by there on our way home from the animal clinic." She seemed more amenable to Charlie's suggestions, at least about getting out of the cold.

Edna frowned as she tried to recall the plan which she'd left on the dashboard of the Kia. Experiencing a momentary lapse of memory, she thought the last two nights of inadequate sleep must be catching up with her. "Animal clinic?"

Gran scowled at her, as if Edna were trying to renege. "We're going by the clinic to pick up Callie."

Now Charlie looked perplexed. "Callie?"

"I adopted one of Laurel's kittens," Gran explained, still staring at Edna as if reminding her of a promise. "A Christmas present for my granddaughter. Roselyn took the cats to the clinic this morning. Said I'd have to go there to finalize the adoption and pick up my little calico."

Her memory jogged, Edna remembered one of the other reasons for coming to CATS and turned to Charlie. "Do you have a list of Laurel's volunteers? Maybe in an address book or a file on her computer? I'd like to call around to see if one of them might have seen or spoken to Mary."

He shook his head. "Laurel's desk was ransacked. Someone broke in through the back door last night, forced the lock. Whoever it was went through the place like a tornado. I haven't found a single personal paper of any sort. Plenty of junk mail, unpaid bills, catalogs, but nothing like a letter or contact information for friends or relatives.

Definitely no address book."

"And her computer?" Edna asked, raising her eyebrows.

"Looks like she had a laptop, but that's missing along with the rest. Whoever took it left only the printer. If she had any thumb drives, those are gone, too. I'm about to canvass the neighborhood to ask if anyone saw or heard anything last night. I also want to find out if anyone recognized the man who was seen in the backyard yesterday afternoon. It's possible he might have been checking out the place and returned last night."

At this suggestion, Edna immediately thought of Vinnie Valmont. Had he been the burglar, trying to recover some money for himself? Perhaps he thought he could get Bethany's back pay, too. Maybe he thought he could sell the computer, if he couldn't find cash. Did he take Bethany to the train so she wouldn't be considered a suspect or an accomplice?

Edna put a hand to her now-pounding head. What was she thinking? Of course, it wasn't Vinnie. With nothing more than her wild imagination to go on, she didn't voice her thoughts. She instinctively liked the young man, but Mary had mentioned he'd been a mischievous youth, in trouble with the police before. He might possibly be a burglar, but a murderer? She mentally shook her head and sought reassurance. "Do you think the person who broke in might be the same one who killed her?"

Before he had a chance to answer, Gran interrupted. "Could we go soon?" Her voice shook with cold, and Edna realized the chill had crept into her own bones, as well.

She instantly felt guilty for keeping the elderly woman outside for so long. The snow had stopped for the time being, but the temperature was dropping fast as the afternoon wore on.

Charlie walked them to the car, holding onto Gran's arm as he helped her through the drifts and around to the passenger's side of the Kia. "Remember, straight home to a pot of tea and a warm fire," he admonished them, but with a half-smile. "Leave the detecting to me." He assisted Gran into the seat while Edna slid behind the wheel and started the engine. Shutting the door, he waved them off. In the rear view mirror, Edna saw him watch as the Kia moved away.

"We're not really going straight home, are we?" Gran's voice still trembled, and she pulled her coat more tightly about herself.

"We'll stop by Perry's clinic first and pick up your kitten." Edna turned to Gran with a conspiratorial look. "And, if the snow holds off, we might as well head over to the hospital. It's not very far out of our way."

As she turned onto the main road that would take them back to town, she was relieved to see it had been freshly plowed and sanded. At the moment, there were few cars, so she thought she and Gran could both use a distraction from the chilly air while the car warmed up.

"I know you're helping out at Krispin's Kitchen because you and Priscilla's mother have been friends since childhood, but how did Codfish McKale come to work there?"

"He was a classmate of ours. Isn't it fun how small the world is sometimes?"

Edna smiled to herself as Gran sat up straighter. The ploy had worked. As she talked, she seemed to forget the cold.

"Walter ... that was his name before he earned his fisherman's stripes." She chuckled at what seemed to be a long-ago memory before continuing. "Walter and I were friends back in our school days. We probably would have started dating, but he dropped out as soon as he turned sixteen. All he ever wanted to do was go to sea." She sighed. "I thought we'd keep in touch, but he was out on the boats from dawn to dusk, sometimes for days on end. When he did get to shore, his mother told me that he'd be so tired, he could hardly keep his eyes open to finish his supper before stumbling off to bed. He came by the house to see me a couple of times, but I was out. He never called or warned me he was coming, you see. I remember he was very shy." She smoothed the collar of her woolen coat away from her neck. The car's heater was doing its job. "I was out with my girlfriends when there wasn't school the next day. Never was one for sitting around the house with my parents. What teenager would?" Sighing, she said, "Eventually, he stopped coming around and we lost track of each other. Since we've reconnected, I've been wondering if I was looking for him in my husbands, all these years."

Remembering that Gran had been twice divorced and once widowed, Edna thought she'd steer the conversation in a slightly different direction. "How did he get nicknamed Codfish?" she asked.

"Oh, that." Gran trilled her delightful, tinkling laugh. "He was a natural fisherman, always knew where to find the best and biggest schools, particularly the cod. Other fishermen christened him with the nickname the day he signed the papers on his first fishing vessel. Proudest day of his life, he told me."

At that thought, she fell silent. She was quiet for so long, Edna finally glanced over to see Gran staring at the windshield. Edna was sure the older woman had gotten lost in thoughts of long-ago times. Eventually, she heaved a sigh and turned to Edna.

"Arthritis caused Walter to give up his boat. He told me he didn't know what to do with himself, once he no longer spent his days trawling the North Atlantic. Faye--that's Priscilla's mother, you know--she told me he spent too much of his time in bars, talking to anyone who'd listen to his tales. Said he'd start singing the old shanties when he had enough whiskey in him."

"So Faye kept in touch with him over the years," Edna guessed.

"No. Their meeting again was pure coincidence. He started eating at the diner. It's the best meal you can get in town for the price. Mostly, you get the daily special or a hamburger plate. Not a lot of variety, but wholesome and filling."

"So Faye recognized him?" Edna asked, not wanting Gran to get sidetracked by the menu.

"Not quite like that. Priscilla got to know him first. She's a good listener and so kind-hearted.

When Walter, or Codfish--I'm trying to get used to that nickname--when he got to know Priscilla, he'd sit for hours telling her his tales of the sea. She'd be sweeping or cleaning up the kitchen while he talked. Eventually, she began handing him a broom or a dish rag as he followed her around."

Edna chuckled at the image. "That sounds like what I used to do when my children wanted to talk. I'd have them help me with whatever cleaning or cooking chore I had to get done at the time."

Gran laughed and then grew serious. "Faye told me Codfish had a pretty bad accident last year and nearly lost his life. Guess it gave him new motivation to live 'cause he's been hanging out at the diner instead of in the bar. He was helping out so much, Priscilla talked to her mother about paying him a small wage. That's when Faye finally met him and realized who he was."

Mention of Codfish's accident made Edna think of Aleda Sharpe, the woman who had sideswiped a drunken Codfish and not stopped. She'd been on her cell phone at the time and, apparently, hadn't known she'd hit the man. After her arrest, Aleda and her husband and their teenage daughter hurriedly left town, amid scandal and gossip. They put their house up for sale and, ironically enough, Gran was the person who bought the property.

"He really hasn't changed much over the years." Gran continued speaking, almost as if to herself. "I think he needs someone to look after him," she said as Edna turned into the parking lot of Perry's Animal Clinic."

Chapter 15

Edna pulled up next to the Perrys' station wagon. She'd barely turned off the engine when she felt suddenly drowsy. She wondered if it might be the over-heated car after she'd been standing out in the freezing cold, or perhaps it was simply her lack of sleep the night before. Whatever the reason, she sat for a moment and closed her eyes.

Apparently oblivious of Edna's weariness, Gran unbuckled her seat belt and opened the passenger-side door. "I bought a carrier and a litter box last week," she said over her shoulder. "Told Carol they were a present for Faye and left them in the car." Her voice made Edna shrug off the fatigue as the older woman slid to the ground and headed around to the rear of the Kia.

When Edna opened her eyes, she was looking directly into a rear window of the clinic where, at that moment, the ghost of a figure seemed to move behind gauzy curtains. She blinked a few times to clear her vision, wondering if what she saw had been a trick of her woozy mind, so ethereal had been the image. It looked as though someone had just ducked below the sill. She stared, waiting to see if the apparition would reappear when Gran's figure moved into her line of sight and broke the trance.

With a shake of her head, Edna got out of the

car. As she did so, she put her hand on the roof of the Perrys' old Volvo to steady herself and glanced down through the passenger-side window where an object on the floor caught her eye. Bending for a closer look, she saw a crushed clump of mistletoe with a bit of red ribbon wrapped around the stem and entangled in the leaves. It looked very much like the "kissing ball" from Laurel's front hall. The last Edna had seen of the decoration was when Laurel was playfully pulling Jake into her house after he and Norm arrived to take Santa photos. She thought of the sprig that Charlie told her had been stuffed into Laurel's teapot and a shiver ran down her spine.

Frowning as she tried to recall the precise image of the ornament Mary had attached to the light fixture, Edna shuffled over the slippery pavement toward the front of the car. She placed her hand on the Volvo's hood to steady herself while she stepped up onto the sidewalk. When she felt warmth through her glove, she also became aware of the soft ticking sound of an engine cooling.

"Something the matter?" Gran was standing on the walk that led to the front door, holding a small plastic pet carrier. "Are you okay, Edna? You look a little pale."

Edna shook her head, uncertain how to answer. Was she so tired she was hallucinating? The image in the window might have been a trick of the light. As for the mistletoe, there were hundreds of such decorations around at this time of year. The warm station wagon meant that at least one of the Perrys was at the clinic. Roselyn, most likely. That would explain the disappearing image in the window. She was so painfully shy, she would not have wanted to be seen. Edna was certain the veterinarian's wife would have a good explanation for the mistletoe in the Volvo, too, if Edna could get the woman to talk to her.

"Sorry to keep you waiting, Gran. I'm okay. Just a touch of fatigue. I had a fitful night, and I think the lack of sleep is catching up with me."

Gran's expression brightened at once. "Then we'll go straight home from here. Charlie was right. We both could use a cup of tea and a rest."

Inside, they were greeted by a young woman in a white lab coat who was sitting behind the reception desk. "Hey, Miz Davies," Jake's intern called. Turning to study the computer screen at her elbow, she wrinkled her brow. "Do we have Benjamin scheduled for today?"

"Hello, Juliana. No, his next visit's not 'til next month." Edna gently drew Gran forward to stand at the waist-high counter beside her. "This is Mrs. Cravendorf. She's adopted a kitten from the CATS shelter. We're here to pick her up."

"Oh, yes, the calico. She's a sweet little munchkin." Juliana rose, grinning. "Roselyn thought you'd be by, so I have the paperwork all ready for you." She reached for a folder and laid it open in front of Gran. "There's information in here for you on the shots she's had and a brochure on care and feeding. If you'll just sign this top form, I'll go get her."

"I brought a carrier." Gran lifted the small crate and handed it across the counter before looking down to examine her adoption materials.

As Juliana accepted the carrier, Edna said, "Is Roselyn available? I'd like to speak with her."

The young woman briefly glanced over her shoulder, almost as if she expected to see someone standing behind her, but then shook her head. "I'm the only one here, right now."

"Oh?" Edna was taken aback. "The Volvo's out front and the engine's still warm. I assumed Roselyn was here." She didn't mention the vision in the window, since she was still uncertain as to what it had been.

Juliana nodded, watching Gran leaf through the pages in the folder. "They left in the van about five or ten minutes ago. Just before you got here." She lifted the small carrier, hugging it against her chest, and finally looked at Edna. "I don't expect them back today. If it's important, I can leave a message and have Roselyn call you."

Had Juliana herself been the figure in the window, Edna wondered, not wanting to question the young woman's word. But the intern had been sitting at the desk when she and Gran had come through the front door. As they'd entered, Juliana had been working at the computer. She hadn't recently rushed from the back room to sit at the desk. Of that, Edna was quite certain.

"I wanted to ask if either Roselyn or Doctor Jake has heard from Mary Osbourne today," Edna said, wishing she could go into the back to make certain nobody else was in the building. The image behind gauzy curtains stuck in her mind.

"Miz Osbourne?" Juliana frowned and paused

for a second or two before shaking her head. "I don't think so. She hasn't phoned the clinic, anyway. She might have called their mobiles, but I wouldn't know about that."

Gran chose that moment to hold up a form. "Is this all you need from me?"

"I have to collect the adoption fee, and there's a charge for shots." Refocusing her attention on Gran, Juliana seemed relieved at the interruption. "The invoice is in the folder with the other papers. Why don't you look it over while I get your kitten," she said, turning to hurry away.

Once the door had closed behind the young woman, Gran put a hand on Edna's forearm. "I'm sorry Roselyn isn't in. It seems to be a wasted trip for you, but I do appreciate your driving me over here to pick up Callie. I'm so excited to get her home. I even lined the carrier and her kitty bed with some old tee-shirts of Carol's. I thought it would help the kitten get used to her new owner."

Edna tried to shake off the feeling that Juliana might be covering for her employer. *I'm being paranoid,* she thought. *Mary's disappearance has me spooked.* She forced herself to concentrate on what Gran was saying.

"Carol will be flying in from Chicago tomorrow afternoon. I can't wait to give her this early Christmas present."

Looking out toward the parking lot, Edna saw the day had darkened. Although it hadn't yet begun to snow again, she thought it probably would before they reached home. *I hope flights won't be cancelled*, she thought, concerned about her own children arriving from Colorado in two days' time, but she wouldn't put a damper on Gran's excitement. "I think the tee-shirts are a wonderful idea. What made you think of it?"

"Something I read. If your cat runs away, you should put a shirt or a towel or something from the laundry basket outside your house. The scent helps them find their way home."

"Yes, I've heard that," Edna nodded in agreement.

"I thought surrounding her with Carol's scent would help Callie adjust more quickly."

"Very clever," Edna said and turned as Juliana came back into the room with Gran's carrier.

"All set. I bet this little one will be glad to get to her permanent home. She's already snuggled into the shirt you put in here."

Gran paid the charges as Edna took the carrier and headed out to the car. She paused to glance into the Volvo and examined the mistletoe once more as she tried to think back to yesterday morning. Was it the mistletoe from Laurel's house? How had it gotten into the Perrys' car? Had Roselyn grabbed it? She remembered Jake had been driving the van yesterday with Norm dressed as Santa Claus, so Roselyn must have been using the station wagon. Could she have ripped the mistletoe from the hall light fixture? She was tall enough. It had been hanging within reach of an average-sized adult. Laurel had told Edna and Mary to hurry and finish when she'd seen the van in the driveway. Maybe in the rush, Mary hadn't secured the mistletoe well enough. Could it have fallen and Roselyn picked it up? If she had, why wouldn't she have left it in the house?

All this speculation was causing Edna's head to pound. Charlie was the one looking into Laurel's death. She should tell him about the mistletoe and concentrate on finding Mary.

After placing the carrier on the back seat of the Kia, she studied the clinic's rear window before climbing in behind the wheel. Gran came out and buckled herself into the passenger's seat, looking as if she had renewed energy, but Edna's fatigue was starting to reassert itself.

"I know we talked about going over to the hospital, but I think you and Charlie are right. I need to get home and put my feet up. I don't think it's really necessary to visit Mary's supervisor in person. I'll phone the hospital later this evening."

This time, when they reached the neighborhood and approached Gran's house, Edna was on the alert for a big, dark vehicle. The road ahead was empty, but as she neared Gran's property, she glanced into the rear view mirror. There it was, less than two car lengths from her bumper. How long had the driver been following her? When she tried to make out his features, once again, fluid sheeted the windshield and the wipers flicked back and forth at full speed. It was impossible for Edna to see who was behind the wheel before she swerved up onto Gran's driveway.

Feeling uneasy about the strange car but not wanting to alarm her companion, Edna silently unloaded the pet supplies from the rear of the Kia. Following Gran as she trudged carefully over the deck with the pet carrier, Edna decided to phone Charlie as soon as she got home.

Gran must have bought out the entire store, Edna thought with some amusement as, a short time later, she assembled a small water fountain and placed it on a rubber mat beside the stainless steel food bowl.

Gran hustled about, setting up a litter box in the small powder room off the kitchen, after which she brought the carrier in and opened the little trap door. "I think it'll be best to let Callie come out when she's ready to explore her new surroundings," she explained as she sat at the kitchen table where she had a direct view of the crate.

Knowing the older woman would be mentally and physically occupied for the evening, Edna declined an invitation to stay for supper, suspecting Gran was only being polite. "I've got to get home to feed my own cat," Edna said as a graceful way to slip out.

The two women arranged that Edna would drive the Kia home and return early the next morning to pick up Gran again. She was working the breakfast shift and had promised Priscilla to arrive by seven o'clock.

When Edna finally walked into the mudroom of her own house, she was truly and thoroughly exhausted. Charlie had apparently gotten hold of the Benton brothers because the brick walk had been shoveled, as had the front stoop. Best of all, the snowpack around her car was gone. *Bless the man*, she thought, and hoped again that Starling would hold onto the detective.

Sinking onto the parson's bench beside the back

door, she greeted Benjamin, talking nonsense to him as she removed her boots, hat and coat. Moving almost mechanically, she fed him, checked his water and shuffled through the kitchen to the living room. As she passed her office door, she noticed the message light blinking on her answering machine. It reminded her that she had planned to call Charlie, but for the life of her, she couldn't remember why at the moment. Her spirits surged when she thought Mary might have left a message, so she hurried to the machine and pressed the button to listen.

"Hello, Mother. It's me. Diane." There was a slight pause as if her daughter expected Edna to pick up. "Father says you're really busy getting everything ready for Grant's visit, so maybe you have the vacuum on and can't hear the phone ring. Anyway, I just called to say Father didn't have to stay in the hospital. Roger and Buddy are helping him to his room and I'm about to make dinner. Call when you can."

"Later," Edna muttered. Once she'd been reassured that Albert was well cared for and out of danger, her energy flagged again. No word from Mary. Dragging her feet, Edna entering the living room. The air was cool, but she had no strength to build a fire. Instead, she pulled an afghan from the back of the sofa, sank into her favorite wingback chair, raised the recliner's footrest and spread the blanket over herself.

*I'll just rest my eyes for a few minutes*, she thought, nestling into the seat.

She was awakened by the grandfather clock chiming the midnight hour. Benjamin was curled up in her lap, and her entire body felt stiff. It seemed to take an agonizingly long time to get upstairs, change into a warm, flannel nightdress and crawl into bed. Whether due to the cold sheets or the long nap she'd had, she drifted in and out of a half-sleep for the next few hours, remembering at one point, through a dim haze, that it was the strange car she needed to call Charlie about, and she should have phoned Albert. She must have fallen deeper into sleep sometime in the wee hours because when the bedside phone rang, she jerked awake, groggy and disoriented.

Chapter 16

"Did I wake you?" Gran sounded more inquisitive than concerned.

Edna rolled over to squint at the bedside clock and nearly groaned aloud when the digital minute flipped at that moment to 6:17.

"I'm sorry, dear, but even if I could drive in this snow, you've got my car. I baked some cinnamon rolls for Priscilla to sample, and I'd like to get to the diner before the breakfast crowd. The Kitchen opens at seven."

*Crowd*, thought Edna, looking out the window at the gently falling snow. *I doubt there'll be a crowd.* Aloud she said, "Give me about twenty minutes and I'll be at your door."

Wanting to stay beneath her warm quilt on this cold winter morning, Edna nonetheless threw back the covers and hurried to the bathroom for a quick, hot shower. Slipping into green wool slacks, yellow turtleneck jersey and a sweater of variegated yarn in rich autumn colors, she nearly ran down the stairs to be greeted by Benjamin. Stopping only to put a fresh scoop of cat chow into his bowl and refresh his water dish, she bundled up in her loden coat and knitted beret. Finally, pulling on calf-high, fur-lined boots and donning mittens, she was ready to brave the morning.

Gran was watching for her from the kitchen window and, as Edna pulled up, walked gingerly across the fresh two inches of snow on the deck. She was carrying a straw basket covered with a red-checkered cloth. When she was safely belted into the passenger's seat of the Kia, she tipped back a corner of the napkin and instantly filled the car with the mouth-watering scent of hot cinnamon sugar.

"Did you and Callie have a good evening," Edna said in greeting.

Gran trilled her infectious laugh. "She crept out only minutes after you left. I followed her all over the house while she explored. She's going to be a wonderful house cat."

Edna drove a little faster than she ordinarily would, considering the falling snow and slick roads, but her head was crying out for coffee and her stomach for breakfast, especially since she'd had no dinner. She parked in front of the cafe where she saw the front walk had been recently shoveled, and mentally noted that there was no lineup of customers waiting to enter. It was just three minutes to seven by the dashboard clock.

The Christmas bells on the door jangled pleasantly when she and Gran stepped into the warmth of the small eatery. Priscilla was sitting on one of the bar stools, leaning back against the counter, holding a cup of coffee in her hands. Vinnie was at the same back table where Edna had sat with him before, a bowl of cereal and a thick porcelain coffee mug in front of him. At the sight of Gran and her basket, Priscilla put down her mug and hurried over.

"You're a doll, as usual, Gran. I've been waiting to try these goodies. Mom says your rolls are the best." She took the basket and kissed the old woman's soft, wrinkled cheek. "Good morning, Edna," she said, turning back toward the counter. Over her shoulder, she called, "How about some coffee and one of these buns?"

"Lovely," Edna called back enthusiastically as she removed her coat and helped Gran off with hers.

"I could use another cup," Gran said, reminding Edna that the woman had probably been up for a while. Where did she get her energy?

Vinnie had been watching while the women greeted each other. When the initial bustle was over, he raised his mug in greeting. "Ladies."

"Hi, Vinnie," Gran said, walking up to his table. "Where's your uncle?"

"I told him I'd pick him up around eight o'clock. I wanted to get the front walk shoveled first."

"Isn't he driving over?"

Vinnie shook his head. "I took his keys." He grimaced, but there was a twinkle in his eye. "I don't want him driving that old rattletrap around with those bald tires. He'll end up in a snow bank and I'll have to go dig him out. Don't tell him, but I'm giving him a tricycle for Christmas. He practically broke his neck learning to ride a two-wheeler a few weeks ago. He liked it, though, so I'm hoping he'll take to the trike. Maybe he won't kill whatever he hits."

Gran laughed and, shaking her head in amusement, went to join Priscilla behind the counter where she was busy with a pair of tongs, taking rolls out of the basket and putting them on small plates.

"These look and smell great. You're still planning on giving me a baking lesson after breakfast, I hope," Priscilla was saying to Gran as Edna approached Vinnie's table.

"May I join you?"

He rose and pulled out a chair for her. "Of course. Let me just grab some rolls for us before Priscilla eats them all," he said, loud enough for the restaurant manager to hear and smile mischievously at him. He turned back to Edna. "Can I bring you some coffee? I'm about to get a warmer. Regular, right?" he asked before moving away.

Edna nodded. "That would be wonderful," she said, sinking onto the chair.

When he returned, he carried two mugs by their handles in one hand and two small plates in the other.

"I think you just saved my life," Edna quipped. She took a sip of hot coffee and began to feel as if she'd survive the day after all. With the fog in her head finally dissipating, she considered again whether Vinnie might have been the one to break into Laurel's house two evenings ago. Certainly, he'd be acting furtive or nervous or guilty. Instead, he seemed friendly, relaxed and innocent.

Tearing off a small piece of breakfast bun, she chewed slowly and tried to think of a way to broach the subject now foremost on her mind.

Vinnie bit into his own roll with relish. He'd finished eating and sat back in his chair, coffee mug held in both hands before Edna spoke. "What time did you say you dropped Bethany off the other night?"

"'Bout six-thirty." He frowned. "Why?"

She remembered very well what time Bethany caught her train because she and Albert had dropped Starling off a few times to catch that same six forty-seven to Boston. What Edna really wanted was to see if she could get Vinnie to admit being in Laurel's back yard. Rather than answer his question, she asked another. "Did either of you see Mary at CATS that afternoon?" She purposely phrased the question in hopes of tricking him into admitting his presence at the shelter.

He scowled as if trying to understand what she was asking. After taking a sip of coffee, he shook his head. "I already told you, I wasn't at CATS. Bethany came by to return my bicycle and asked if I'd drive her to the train. She never mentioned Mary. Why are you asking about her anyway? Doesn't she live next door to you?"

Edna shrugged as if it didn't matter. If Vinnie were lying, he deserved a Thespian award. She couldn't tell him the real reason for her questions without alienating him, so she gave a purposely vague answer. "I haven't seen her lately and wondered when you or Bethany might have spoken to her last. I want to ask her a few things about her Christmas Eve party." At least that was the truth. She certainly wanted to ask Mary why she wasn't home getting ready for her guests.

"Oh, the party," Vinnie said, sitting forward and picking up his empty plate. His eyes brightened. "I got an invitation. So did Codfish." He rose.

"Speaking of the old man, I'd better go get my uncle before he gets antsy and decides to hot-wire his truck."

Edna felt a flash of panic. She sensed he might have information important to finding Mary, but she didn't know exactly what that might be or what questions to ask to draw it out of him. Charlie was sending someone to speak to Bethany, and Edna didn't want to get in the way of a police investigation, but she couldn't sit around waiting. If she couldn't pin Vinnie down, she'd have to talk to Bethany. Edna held up a hand to delay Vinnie. "Before you go, would you give me Bethany's phone number?"

"Sure." He went behind the counter to put his plate and coffee mug on the shelf of the pass-through and returned a moment later to give Edna a paper napkin on which he'd scribbled a phone number. "That's her cell," he said as he lifted a ski jacket off the back of his chair. "See ya later." Still pulling on the jacket, he went out through the front door to the sound of the jangling bells.

Edna was about to take out her own cell phone to call the young woman when she heard sounds of banging and clanging coming from the kitchen. Before she could get up to investigate, a matronly woman in a long black wool coat pushed open the double swinging doors. A black knit cap was pulled down nearly to her brows.

"I need help unloading supplies," she called into the room.

Gran and Priscilla were standing before the cash register and hadn't bothered to turn at the din.

Deeply engrossed, Priscilla seemed to be showing Gran how to work the credit card machine.

"Hello, Mother," she called without turning around. "Be with you in a minute."

"Never mind," Edna said, rising and gathering up her dishes. "I'll help." Heading toward the woman, she introduced herself and said, "You must be Faye Krispin. I've heard so much about you from Gran." There was something familiar about the woman, Edna thought, turning to put her dirty dishes next to Vinnie's on the pass-through counter. Puzzling over where she might have seen the woman before, she said, "I'll get my coat."

Spinning back into the kitchen, Faye said, "Come through this way. My car's out back. I'll meet you there."

A few minutes later, Edna stepped through the door to the rear parking lot. Faye was in the process of lifting a box from the back seat of a bright blue sedan. Glancing down at the license plate, Edna saw the last two numbers were a three and a two. Now she knew why the woman looked familiar. She had nearly knocked Edna down rushing out of Laurel Taylor's house three mornings ago.

Chapter 17

"What do you want to know about that wicked woman?" Faye asked once she and Edna were seated at the back table. She had said she'd be willing to talk to Edna, but not before she'd gotten the supplies out of her car and into the kitchen. The snow was still coming down, and she didn't want to delay the unloading. As they had worked, Edna briefly explained to Faye that she'd been one of the women on the porch when Faye had stormed out of Laurel's house.

Looking slightly abashed, Faye said, "I was vaguely aware of bumping into someone. You say that was you?" She had stopped to look at Edna after lifting a carton of lettuce and vegetables from the car. "I do apologize, but I was rather upset. I'm afraid I wasn't myself."

"No harm done," Edna said, leaning in to pick up the last grocery bag before closing the trunk's lid. By the time she turned, Faye had already disappeared into the building.

Once finished, Edna followed Faye into the main dining room and was surprised to see customers occupying one of the tables and three of the stools at the counter. She realized it was the first time she'd been in the restaurant when they were open for business. Priscilla was busy preparing breakfast plates while Gran waited on the four customers. Instead of coffee, Edna and Faye each prepared tea for themselves, carrying their mugs to the table. Edna purposely chose to sit in Vinnie's usual chair, facing the room, so Faye would look at her and not be distracted by the patrons.

"How did you know Laurel?" Edna replied to Faye's query.

The woman narrowed her eyes at Edna, looking at her with obvious suspicion. Faye seemed to be as straightforward and no-nonsense as her childhood friend Gran. "Why do you want to know about her? What has she to do with you?"

Edna thought for a minute, unsure how to answer. Hesitantly at first, but becoming more certain as she spoke, she said, "A friend of mine is missing. She was last seen leaving CATS the afternoon Laurel died. I think her disappearance has something to do with the death. She may have seen what happened. If she did, a killer may be after her … or worse." Edna finally spoke what she had forced to the back of her mind until that moment, not wanting to bring the unthinkable into conscious thought. She could ignore her fears no longer.

Faye's expression turned from suspicion to horror. "I'm sorry about your friend." Her look morphed into anger, and she went on, "As for Laurel Taylor, she was a bad woman. She didn't deserve to die, but I can't help thinking her past finally caught up with her."

"What do you mean by that?"

"I mean she's a liar and a thief."

"A thief?" It wasn't quite what Edna had

expected to hear, but her curiosity certainly was piqued.

"You bet she was. She stole my brother's life savings."

Edna was instantly alert. She knew enough by now to realize that the more you learned about a victim, the closer you came to unveiling a murderer. She hadn't had much success, so far, in trying to follow Mary's trail, so perhaps if she discovered the identity of Laurel's killer, maybe she'd find Mary. Edna didn't dare imagine what shape her friend would be in by this time. She'd been missing for nearly two days. "Would you please begin at the beginning and tell me everything you know about Laurel?"

Faye slowly bounced her teabag in the mug of hot water, but her mind seemed far away. Nearly a minute passed before, twining the string around a spoon, she squeezed water from the bag and laid both it and the spoon aside. After taking a sip of the brew, she began her story.

"Bob--that's my brother--Bob lives alone in a small house on the outskirts of Bloomington, Indiana." She gave Edna a weak smile. "I guess he's not entirely alone. He has a dog. Heidi's a Golden, a real sweetie."

Edna nodded understanding before asking, "How did your brother meet Laurel?"

"She called herself a 'health companion.' Two years ago, he fell and broke his wrist. He didn't want to go to a rehab center which would also mean putting Heidi in a kennel while he recuperated, so he advertised for some temporary help. Making a long story short, Laurel was one of the women who answered his ad, and he hired her. When his wrist had healed and he was able to do for himself, instead of leaving, she stayed on. Bob's house is small, but there's a back room next to the downstairs bathroom off the kitchen. It had been a junk room before he had it cleaned out and converted to a bed-sitting room for live-in help. He said he got used to having someone else in the house. He liked it that Laurel would clean and cook when he didn't feel like it. If you ask me, I think he got used to having a woman wait on him again. He'd been a widower for seven years before his accident, you know."

Edna didn't know, but kept silent, waiting for Faye to continue.

"Apparently, Laurel stayed to herself most of the time, kept to her room when she wasn't out buying groceries or running some sort of errand for Bob. Since she was living in the house and eating his food, once he was able to look after himself, he didn't have to pay her anything. Room and board was more than enough, if you want my opinion."

"Why did she stay on?" Edna asked. "Didn't she need to earn spending money, at least?"

Faye shrugged and took another sip of tea, wincing as she did so. "Cold," she said, making a face and putting the mug to one side. She picked up a paper napkin and twisted it between her fingers as she continued her story.

"Bob says she didn't talk much about herself, but from the way she acted at times and from things she'd say now and then, he got the feeling she was hiding from someone. He supposed she wanted a place to live where she didn't have to put stuff in her name--you know, like utilities and such." Faye scowled. "Wish I'd known at the time. I'd have found out what was going on. Must be something wrong with a person who needs to hide out."

Thinking of Carol James and the situation that made her hide from mobsters, Edna didn't agree with Faye's conclusion, but said nothing. Evidently, Gran hadn't filled her friend in on Carol's plight, so Edna certainly wasn't going to say anything. Instead, she prompted Faye to go on with her brother's situation. "So what happened? You said Laurel stole your brother's life savings?"

"I have to back up to the beginning to explain," Faye said, beginning to shred the napkin in her hands. Anger and resentment were clear in her tone. "When Bob's wrist was in the cast, he couldn't write, of course. Laurel made out his checks, opened his mail, things like that, so she knew what his financial situation was. Most of his savings he had in stocks and bonds. He'd had the same broker for years, recommended by his accountant, and had no complaints. The portfolio wasn't making Bob much money, but he wasn't losing it, either. Until *she* came along." Faye made "she" sound like a hiss of disgust as her face contorted with renewed rage.

Edna reached across the table and gently squeezed Faye's hand, hoping to calm the woman. Faye took a deep breath and bowed her head for several seconds before taking another deep breath and smiling sadly at Edna.

"I know my brother is partly to blame. He's a

kind and an honest man. I think that might be why he tends to trust people. His friends have never before taken advantage of his compassion, so that's another reason I think he trusted Laurel. He hasn't said as much, but knowing Bob, I bet he figured he could get her to open up, tell him what she was scared of, and then help her. After she took his money and ran away, he said he probably should have noticed a change in her, but he had been lulled into complacency by that time. He never thought she'd cheat him after being with him for two years."

"Something must have caused her to act as she did. Does he know what that was?" Edna was intrigued.

"I'm getting to that." Apparently, Faye wanted to tell the story in her own time and in her own way. "Somehow, Laurel convinced Bob that his broker wasn't doing such a good job handling his money. She said she knew someone who could do better. Don't ask me why, but instead of having his money transferred, he went along with Laurel's suggestion and instructed his broker to send a certified check to him by registered mail."

"And Laurel intercepted the check," Edna guessed.

Faye nodded. "The day the check arrived, that woman met the postman coming up the walk. She was sweeping the porch. It's obvious now that she'd been waiting for him. By that time, she knew all the delivery people, of course, and they were used to her signing for my brother. She told the postman that Bob wasn't home. That was true enough." Faye snorted derisively. "She'd sent him into the city on a fool's errand. Had him go into the city to an Italian deli that she said had the best ingredients for a special dinner she wanted to make for him. It also happened to be near a place he could hike with Heidi off leash." Faye shook her head sadly. "She knew he'd be gone most of the afternoon. He loved to see his dog run free. Well, sure enough, when he got home late that afternoon, she'd cleared out--bag, baggage and his life savings."

"How did you find her? Isn't it a little coincidental that she ended up here in Rhode Island, near you? Did she know that members of Bob's family live in this area?"

"He and I talked about that. Once we found out more about her, we thought it made some sort of warped sense for her to hide close to her husband's family."

More than a little confused, Edna repeated her earlier question. "How did you find her?"

"We hired a detective. At first, Bob didn't want to spend the money, but I told him Priscilla and I would help with some of the profits from the diner. When he found her and got his money back, he could reimburse us if he wanted to."

Remembering the autopsy report that indicated Laurel had been an abused wife, Edna was more than a little curious about the woman's husband. "Did you say her husband's family also live around here?"

Faye nodded at the same time she must have realized what a mess she'd made of the napkin. She spoke to the tabletop as she began to sweep together shreds of paper with the side of her hand. "As part of his investigation, our private detective found out that Laurel was married and had run away from her husband about the time she answered Bob's ad for a caregiver. She was originally from Texas, around Fort Hood, so the detective checked with the army. Sure enough, he found her marriage license and was able to trace the husband--or his family, at least. Surprised us all to learn that her in-laws live so close to me and Priscilla. Our best guess is that maybe she thought she could squeeze money out of them, too, somehow." Faye looked up at Edna and scowled. "Who knows what sort of twisted logic runs through the head of a person like that."

Edna knew it was a rhetorical question and paid no attention to it as she felt her excitement grow. "Who is this family?" Her head was whirling with the implications. What if Mary had learned about them and their relationship to Laurel? She would be like a bloodhound following a scent. Would she confront them? In her pursuit, could she have forgotten about everything else, including the fact that tomorrow evening was Christmas Eve and her big party?

At that moment, the door opened to admit four new customers followed by Vinnie and Codfish. When Edna glanced up at the commotion, she saw that Gran was busy at the register and looked frazzled as she hovered over the credit card machine. Two customers, waiting in line to pay their checks, were obviously growing impatient.

"Mother, could you please come help?" Priscilla appeared from the kitchen balancing two plates of eggs and pancakes on her left arm and holding a pot of coffee in her right hand. She, too, looked harried. Having caught her mother's attention, Priscilla immediately turned to Vinnie and jerked her head toward the kitchen in silent appeal before serving her patrons.

Edna and Faye had been so absorbed in the story of Laurel Taylor that they'd failed to notice the diner filling up.

Faye immediately jumped up, dropped the shredded napkin bits into her tea mug and hurried off toward the kitchen. Left alone, Edna realized not only were the newest arrivals staring at her, obviously hoping to have her seat, but they were also brushing a layer of snow from their shoulders. She knew she would be of no help around the diner, having not a single clue of what to do, but she had plenty of work waiting for her at home. She was grabbing her coat off the back of her chair, as Vinnie came from the kitchen to bus the table.

"Would you tell Gran to call me when she's ready to leave? I'll come back and pick her up."

"No need for that, Miz Davies," he said. "I can drive her home."

Feeling relieved that she needn't worry about Gran, frustrated that her talk with Faye had been interrupted for the time being, and anxious about the mounting snow, Edna left the café.

## Chapter 18

The snow was coming down steadily and persistently. Fortunately, the wind wasn't strong, so driving was slow, but not particularly hazardous. With only half her concentration on the road, Edna was able to plan what she had to do when she reached the house. Since she'd not spoken to Albert last night, that item was first on her mental list. She'd also have to call Charlie and let him know about the mistletoe she'd seen in the Perrys' Volvo. As she approached her neighborhood, her attention switched to the side roads and driveways as she passed each one. She must tell Charlie about the strange vehicle that had twice nearly run her off the road.

She was so absorbed in trying to remember all that she had to report to the detective, at first she thought she was hallucinating when she spotted Charlie's car parked behind her own and the man himself standing by the wire-framed sleigh in the middle of the circular driveway. He was staring up at the chimney, but he lowered his gaze and waved as she stopped behind his unmarked police sedan and slid out of the Kia.

"I thought you were home and refusing to let me in," he joked, tugging his collar up around his neck against the snow as he approached. "Isn't this

Carol's car?"

She nodded, hunching into her own coat. "I'm chauffeuring Gran around. She doesn't feel safe driving in snow, now that she's used to Florida winters. I've been glad of the use of it since Kevin plowed my car in." As she spoke, Edna realized that the driving she'd done had all been for her neighbor, otherwise she'd have been able to stay home and prepare for her family's arrival.

"Well, you're unstuck now. I see the Benton boys got my message and did some shoveling around here."

"Yes, thank you for arranging it. I'll get hold of them soon to pay them, but tell me, what are you doing here? Have you heard from Mary?" Her heart lifted in anticipation.

He scowled. "No. No word yet. One of the reasons I stopped by was to ask you the same question."

She shook her head. "What about Bethany? Any word from Boston?"

It was Charlie's turn to shake his head. "Afraid not. My friend on the force will be going over there this morning. I hope to hear from him by lunchtime."

Feeling helpless and more than a little concerned about Mary, Edna said, "Let's get out of this weather. I've learned some things lately that you should know about."

As they rounded the car, Charlie motioned with his chin toward the roof. "Did you notice that Santa has deflated?" He grimaced. "I was afraid this snow might be too heavy for the old guy. I can't tell you how many years I've had that balloon man." He checked his watch. "I can't spare the time right now, but I'll come back this evening with my ladder to get him down. Maybe I can repair him." He offered his arm and helped her through the snow

As they trudged along the brick path to the back door, she said, "Have you any more news on Laurel Taylor?"

"I managed to track her back to her last job. Seems she was working for some old guy in Indiana."

Edna smiled to herself, pleased to be able to fill in some blanks for Charlie's investigation. "Well, I have more information than that for you. I know who that 'old guy' is. I've just left his sister."

Charlie snorted a laugh. "How do you do it, Edna?"

She grinned up at him. "It was pure coincidence. Since this has to do with your investigation, surely you can stay a while. I'll make a pot of coffee and tell you what I've learned. Also, I think I have something pertinent to your borrowed-bicycle mystery."

Benjamin was waiting at the door as soon as Edna stepped into the mudroom. Before Charlie could slip inside, the ginger cat poked his head out. The two humans watched with some amusement as he inspected the falling flakes and the mounds of icy, cold snow building up on the ground. Rather than venture out, he gave a clear sneeze of disgust and returned to his bed.

At the kitchen table, over a fresh pot of coffee and a plate of warmed-up biscuits with homemade strawberry jam, Edna told Charlie about Faye and her brother Bob. She finished by admitting, "We were interrupted before Faye gave me the husband's name or his family's."

"I'll stop by the diner and speak to Faye myself. We'll locate the relatives," Charlie said. "This is a good lead, Edna, but you need to be careful. You know what happened last time you got mixed up in a murder." He didn't need to elaborate, but he did add with a lighter tone, "If anything happened to you, Starling would never forgive me."

His warning stirred memories that made Edna shiver. "I don't ever want to be in that sort of danger again, believe me, but I don't think talking to Faye falls into that category. I don't think trying to locate Mary does either. Do you?"

He shook his head. "It wouldn't seem so, but you'd still better leave the detecting to me." Before she could take umbrage at this comment, he looked at his watch and pushed his chair back from the table. "I need to be off, but you said you had something relevant to the missing bicycles."

She nodded. "Have you seen a big, dark car in this neighborhood lately? It looks like one of those square military things."

"You mean a Humvee?" He looked thoughtfully at her for several seconds before answering. "No. Can't say as I have. Why? What has this to do with the bicycles?"

"I'm just guessing, but ..." Edna told him what she could remember about the car and explained what had happened twice now when she'd been heading to Gran's house. She ended by saying,

"And the strangest thing is, the driver turns on the windshield wipers and sprays washer fluid each time he gets near enough for me to get a good look at him." She crumbled the edge of an untouched biscuit on her plate, concentrating on her fingers while she put her thoughts together. Looking up at Charlie, she concluded, "I'm probably making something out of nothing, but it made me think of your mystery and the tracks you saw the other morning. Now that the snow makes it impossible to ride a bike on the road, I wonder if the driver of that car might be the same person cruising our neighborhood and maybe looking for Carol."

"Did you get a plate number?"

She shook her head. "I was so busy trying to avoid an accident, I didn't even think to look at the plates."

"That's okay," Charlie said. "I'll alert the patrol and have them keep an eye out." He took a notebook out of his pocket. "You say it was a dark-colored Humvee."

"Yes, if that's what those military-looking things are called. I'm pretty certain it's black, but it might be dark blue. With that fluid all over the windshield, I couldn't make out who was driving. Just a silhouette. I'm not even certain it was a man. I'm sorry but that's all I can tell you."

"I'll call it in. If you see it again, call me right away."

As soon as he left, Edna picked up the phone and dialed Albert's cell. To her surprise, Diane answered.

"Where's your father?"

"He's still sleeping."

Edna looked at the clock. "He doesn't usually sleep past eight in the morning."

"His body needs more rest while it's healing," came the reply from her nurse-trained daughter.

"Why are you answering his phone?"

"I took it last night, after he fell asleep. I didn't think he should be disturbed."

"Isn't that his call … if you'll pardon the expression?" Edna figured her daughter probably wouldn't understand the humor, but Edna was trying hard not to scold. She paused to take a deep breath, remembering this was the child who meant well. *It's just that she goes a bit too far, sometimes*, Edna thought. Instead of speaking her mind, she said, "How is he feeling? What did the doctors say about his heart?"

"His tests show that his heart is fine. His blood pressure is lower than the doctor would like, but Father took it easy yesterday. He's to rest and not get upset."

*You don't think he'll be upset when he finds out you've taken his phone?* Edna swallowed the retort. Aloud, she asked after Diane and the rest of the family, simply to make small talk.

"We're doing well, thank you, Mother. We're looking forward to Mary's open house tomorrow evening. It's been wonderful having Father here, but I know he'll be happy to get home. He doesn't want to be a burden on you. That's why he's overdoing his exercises, trying to build up his strength too quickly."

If Edna was supposed to comment on this remark

or feel guilty as the cause of Albert's setback, she couldn't think of a soothing thing to say. "Please tell him I phoned and give him my love. I'd like to chat more with you, dear, but I've still got lots to do. I'll see you tomorrow afternoon." As she hung up, she thought, *There may not be a party tomorrow, if Mary doesn't show up soon.*

Glancing at the desk clock and trying to ignore the pile of Christmas cards she had yet to address, Edna noted it wasn't quite nine o'clock, which meant it would be not quite seven in Colorado. Early, she thought, but someone is bound to be up with the baby. Dean slept well, but went to bed early and was usually awake by six. It was with this thought she dialed Grant's home number, expecting Karissa to answer, so was both pleased and surprised when Grant picked up.

"Hello, Mother."

"Hello, dear. How was your skiing trip?"

"Incredible, but we cut it short. We've been catching the Rhode Island weather reports. It sounds like you're having quite a storm."

Edna turned to look out the window of her small office and saw large snowflakes drifting past the glass. "It's snowing at the moment, but it's been doing this for a couple of days, now. Just when I think we'll get a foot or more, it stops for a while," she said, hoping that would be the case with the latest flurries.

"We'll be following the airport news today. We're all looking forward to a New England Christmas, and a white one will be awesome. Rhode Island snow is much better for making snowmen than Colorado powder. Can't wait to show the kids."

"And I can't wait to see all of you, dear." Edna's heart lifted again at the thought of her family together for the holiday. Remembering the main reason for her call to Colorado, she said, "I haven't gotten a crib for Dean yet and am wondering ..."

She didn't have time to finish the sentence before Grant cut in. "Didn't Karissa tell you? We're bringing his portable with us. It's much more compact and easier than setting up an entire crib. He'll be fine."

Mentally chiding herself for not thinking to mention a crib before, Edna chatted with her son for a few more minutes before they hung up with words of "love to everyone" and "see you tomorrow."

She spent the rest of the morning preparing the rooms for Grant's family. She thought nine-year-old Jillian would bunk in with Starling. Dean could share the room with his parents. Shaking her head in amusement at Albert's suggestion that the bottom drawer of the chest would suffice for a fourteen-month-old, she sighed with relief that a big item had been removed from her to-do list.

The pleasure she felt over the arrival of her children and grandchildren was shattered when her thoughts abruptly turned to Mary. Where was she? Would she be home in time for her party tomorrow night? Was she even able to get home?

"Where could she be and why doesn't she call?" Edna asked Benjamin as he watched her put clean towels on the racks in the guest bathroom. He sat on the edge of the tub and only stared at her with unblinking green eyes. As if her thoughts had conjured up the action, the phone rang. Ready to believe it had to be Mary, Edna raced to the bedroom and picked up the extension.

"Hello? Mary?"

"No, Edna. It's Gran." After a second's pause, she said with evident excitement, "Have you heard from Mary? Were you expecting a call from her?"

"Oh, hi, Gran." Edna tried to keep the disappointment from her voice. "She was on my mind when the phone rang, so it was only wishful thinking." With a sinking heart both because the caller wasn't Mary and because Edna hadn't expected to go back out into the snow that afternoon, she said, "Do you need me to come get you?"

"No, dear. Vinnie brought me home an hour ago. I was phoning to give you some bad news, I'm afraid."

Edna felt like hanging up right then, but she couldn't be that rude to Gran. Determined to be a good sport, whatever the news, she said, "Not too bad, I hope."

"Carol just phoned to say her flight from Chicago has been cancelled. She won't get home today. Apparently, they haven't been able to clear the runways or de-ice the planes fast enough to keep up with the scheduled flights."

Edna thought she heard a catch in Gran's voice and knew how disappointed she felt. Edna herself was feeling as if all the air had been sucked out of her. What if her children's flight was cancelled tomorrow? She felt sick, but managed to perk up enough to say, "Don't worry, Gran. I'm sure Carol will be home tomorrow." But Edna wasn't at all certain of that. Aiming for a cheerful note, she asked, "How's little Callie adjusting to her new home?" With Gran's delighted reply, the two women spoke for a minute more before hanging up. Edna went back to her chores, trying very hard not to think about cancelled flights and closed airports. She would hope for the best. Of course her children would make it home for Christmas. She would not jinx the holiday by thinking otherwise.

Seven o'clock that evening found her in her small office. Relieved to have crossed most of the tasks off her to-do list, she was finally sitting down to her Christmas cards. Many of her far-away friends and family members wouldn't be receiving season's greetings until after the fact, but at least she would reach those with whom she corresponded only once a year. When the phone rang at her elbow, the sound made her hand jerk, scratching a thin, inky-blue line across the "Holiday Wishes" to the top of the card she'd just begun.

"Drat," she muttered. She'd have to throw it away and begin her message anew. She was reaching for the receiver on the third ring when the doorbell chimed. She first answered the call with a hurried "Hello."

"Is this Edna Davies?" an unrecognized woman's voice asked over the line.

"Yes, this is she."

"This is Faye Krispin." After a half-second hesitation, she added, "from the Kitchen."

"Oh, yes, Faye. Someone came to the door just

as I picked up your call. Can you hold a moment?"
Before the woman could reply, Edna put down the
receiver and had stepped from the office when the
caller began to bang heavily and repeatedly on the
door.

"Hold your horses. I'm coming," she nearly
shouted into the empty hall.

The sound of the bell had roused Benjamin from
the chair beside the desk where he slept whenever
she worked in the office. Jumping down, he
preceded her into the hall and waited while she
opened the door.

"Evenin', Miz Davies. Hope I'm not disturbing
you." Kevin Lockhorn stood on the front stoop,
inside the storm door which she'd apparently left
unlocked. He slipped past her into the hall as he
spoke.

Trying to be polite and hide her astonishment at
his intrusion, she shut the front door and moved past
him. "I'll be with you in a minute, Kevin," she
called over her shoulder. "I'm on the phone."
Almost unconsciously and a second before she
reentered her office, she noticed that Benjamin had
disappeared. "Hello, Faye. Are you still there?"

"I won't keep you, but you seemed anxious to
know Laurel Taylor's husband's family's name."

"Yes, I am." Edna picked up her pen and reached
for a scrap of paper to jot down whatever
information Faye was about to impart.

"It's Greene. The uncle was Thomas McKinley
Greene. When we tried to reach him, we learned
that he had died, but a daughter and grandson live in
the area, as well as a cousin. Laurel's husband's

name was Kevin Lockhorn."

## Chapter 19

Edna nearly dropped the phone as she sensed Kevin's presence in the hallway. Was he behind her? The hair on the back of her neck bristled at the thought. Was he listening?

"Thank you, Mrs. Krispin. I've made a note of it. Thank you for calling."

She hung up, hoping the quiver she felt along her spine was not apparent in her voice. For appearance sake, she wrote a few words on the scrap of paper as if it were an appointment. Only then did she feel calm enough to turn around with the confidence to smile and greet her visitor. He wasn't in the doorway as she had expected. Stepping into the hall, she didn't see him there, either. She glanced into the kitchen before heading for the living room. *Where was he?*

As she walked through the archway into the living room, she saw him standing next to the Christmas tree. He held Danny's present in one hand, slapping the tube against the open palm of the other as, head cocked to one side, he examined the tree. She realized again how much he resembled his uncle--a big man, fit and strong. Physical similarities were where the likeness ended, apparently. Kevin had been in the army, so he must have been combat trained. Her heart thudded as she realized, alone in the house, she'd be defenseless if he became violent. Charlie's words popped into her head--*Couple of broken ribs, older than the arm fracture. Her collar bone has been broken, too.*

She moved to stand behind her wingback chair and gripped the top to steady herself. She wondered if he intended to hit her with the cardboard tube.

"Please put that down. You'll tear the wrapping." The night of her trimming party, she had forgotten to give Danny's present to Kevin and had felt badly that the boy wouldn't receive his grandfather's portrait until after Christmas. Now, she had another reason for wishing it had left the house that evening. A cardboard tube wouldn't be lethal, but it could certainly hurt and humiliate.

Ignoring Edna's request, Kevin kept his eyes on her, turning only his head as she'd moved across the room. He grinned disarmingly. "Hope you don't mind. I made myself at home. I thought I'd visit our Christmas tree while you finished your phone call. We did a pretty good job of decorating it, don't you think?" He pivoted to face her, lowering Danny's present to smack it rhythmically against his pant leg. "Nice party the other night, by the way."

The words spoken in a soothingly gentle tone, so contrary to his behavior, increased her unease. She balked at his possessive "our" for her family's tree, but brushed it aside. Trying not to show fear, she said, "I don't mean to be rude, Kevin, but is there something in particular you wanted to see me about? Tomorrow is the last day before Christmas, and I have a ton of cards to write this evening."

His grin faded as he sauntered to the fireplace

and stared down at the glowing embers behind the screen for a few seconds. Only the chair stood between them now. She wondered if he would throw Danny's present into the fire. When his eyes lifted to hers, they seemed filled with suspicion. "Actually, I'm looking for Mary. I thought she might be here." As if swapping favor for favor, he twisted his shoulders and gently tossed the wrapped tube so that it landed and rolled beneath the tree.

Surprised and momentarily silenced by the action, Edna stared at him for several heartbeats before responding. "I think you can see for yourself that I'm quite alone." Edna's instincts warned her not to reveal that she, too, was looking for Mary.

This man had been Laurel Taylor's husband. Was he abusive? Had he been the one to beat her, leaving evidence of broken bones that the medical examiner found? Kevin looked so much like his uncle Tom, she wanted to believe he was as gentle and kind. On the other hand, Norm Wilkins, their cousin, had a mile-long mean streak. Did Kevin take after that branch of the family? These thoughts were spinning around in her head while the man in front of her studied her face with narrowing eyes. Tightening her grip on the chair back and hoping he wouldn't see her fingers tremble, she waited for him to speak.

"Aren't you good friends, you and Mary?" His tone hinted at a growing impatience.

She nodded. "We are."

"Then you know where she is." The statement was matter-of-fact, leaving no trace of doubt in the accusation.

There was no use arguing with a man whose mind was already made up. Partly to distract him and somewhat out of curiosity, she asked, "Why did you pack the snow around my car yesterday?"

He chuckled, looking pleased with himself. "You wouldn't answer the door. Didn't you hear me knock? I banged hard enough."

"I wasn't home," she said, adding silently, *And thank goodness for that*.

"Your car was out front." He stated the fact as if it were proof that she was lying.

"Is that why you blocked it in, because you thought I was hiding behind my curtains?" She felt her own temper begin to rise. What a childish thing for a grown man to do.

"Nah. I did it 'cause I didn't want you to leave before I had a chance to talk to you. I had another job to get to, but it wasn't going to take long. I was going to dig your car out after we talked."

"Were you looking for Mary then, too, or did you have another reason for ensuring I stayed home?"

At once, he became less belligerent and said almost pleadingly, "It's really important. I gotta talk to Mary"

"About what?" Edna was more curious than angry now.

"Not your business." His face reddened slightly. He sounded as if he were about to lose patience again. As he started to move around the chair, a faint noise from the hall caught his attention. "What was that? Who else is in the house? Thought you said you were alone."

She hesitated for only a second. "I have a cat. He's probably knocked over something on the kitchen shelf."

But she knew Benjamin better than that. He wouldn't be up on the counters. Her heart skipped a beat as she herself wondered who else was in the house. Her back prickled as she remembered the last man who had entered her house uninvited. That man was in jail, but there might be others out looking for Carol James. Was it the man in the Humvee? She wanted to turn so her back wasn't to the unknown in the hallway, but then she wouldn't be facing Kevin.

While she had been distracted by these thoughts, Kevin had moved to her side. He grabbed her elbow and squeezed as he growled, "Where is she?"

"I'm right here, Kevin. Let her go."

They both spun around at the sound of Mary's voice. The tall red-head seemed to have materialized in the doorway, so silently had she appeared. Wearing a white camouflage coverall patterned with what appeared to be tree branches, she had wrapped her red hair completely in a scarf of the same cloth. Since she didn't have the girth of a snowman, she looked more like a winter scarecrow, with only a pale, narrow face and brilliant green eyes standing out in the fabric. Benjamin sat behind her, quiet and watching, his eyes on Kevin.

In that split second, Edna also noticed that Mary was turned slightly sideways, her right arm down by her side and her hand hidden behind her thigh. Edna recognized the pose and knew Mary held a gun.

"Mary?" was all Edna could manage to gasp, making the name into a question. Torn between relief at seeing her friend and anxiety at what was obviously tension between Mary and Kevin, Edna couldn't think of anything to say. Where to begin? She had so many questions.

"What are you doing here?" Mary broke the growing silence, her eyes never leaving Kevin's face.

"I've been looking for you. We need to talk."

"Nothing to talk about, far as I can tell. I saw you run from Laurel's house two days ago. Did you kill her?"

Edna took in a sharp breath and looked at Kevin. His face was bright red now. She didn't think it was from the fire's heat.

"Are you crazy?" The words burst from his throat, almost a growl. "I never saw her. She refused to open the door." He slid his eyes to Edna before glaring back at Mary. "That the way you women treat people in these parts?"

"Why were you sneaking around her backyard?" Mary asked, clearly not believing his story. "If you wanted to see her, why not walk in the front door. It's not even locked during the day."

"I didn't want anyone to see me."

Mary scoffed. "Why not? If you're so innocent, why were you acting so guilty?"

He glowered for several seconds, as if making up his mind to something. "She's got a restraining order. I'm not supposed to go near her."

"Is that why you ran when I called out? You were violating a restraining order?" She snorted derisively. "I'm not that stupid, Kevin. Those orders are ignored more often than not."

"All I know is I heard a car coming up her driveway, so I took off for my truck. I saw you at the stop sign, but until then, I didn't know it was you who yelled at me. How'd you get around the corner so fast?" Without waiting for a reply, he went on. "Even when I recognized you in that ragtop of yours, I wasn't about to stop in that neighborhood. Like I told you, I wasn't supposed to go anywhere near her." He stopped talking and glared at Mary as if daring her to doubt him.

"You expect me to believe you didn't go into the house?"

"That's why I've been looking for you. I wanted to talk to you, to convince you I had nothing to do with my wife's death."

Edna noticed the surprise that flashed across Mary's face and wondered if Kevin had seen it, too. Apparently, this was the first she'd heard of Kevin's relationship to Laurel. True to form, Mary's recovery was instant, but before she could speak, another voice was heard.

"Talk to *me*, Kevin. I'm the one you need to convince," Charlie said, stepping out of the shadows to stand beside Mary.

The relief that swept over Edna was enormous. She felt faint with the rush and reached out to grab the chair back. He was wearing jeans and a pullover that had seen better days. She supposed he had come by to remove his deflated Santa Claus from the roof. Whatever the reason, she was happy to see him. Maybe he could dispel the almost-physical feeling of tension between Mary and Kevin.

Charlie stood silently for a minute. When Kevin only stared back at him, the detective's glance moved to Edna. Studying her face, he asked quietly, "You okay?" She nodded, unable to speak. His eyes shifted to follow the line of Mary's arm from her shoulder to her hand. "Put it away," he said, sounding almost amused, but not quite. "Make sure the safety's on."

"Never took it off." Mary grinned at him as she brought her hand into sight of the others in the room. Looking insolently at Kevin, she moved her feet slightly apart to stand like a soldier at ease, only her wrists were crossed in front of her and one hand gripped the pistol.

Kevin glared accusingly at Mary. "What'd you call in the cavalry for? There was no need for that."

Before she could answer, Charlie said, "I'm the one you need to talk to, Kevin."

"I didn't kill Laurel. I don't know how else to say it," he said stubbornly. "How do I convince you I'm innocent?"

"Why did you break into the house?" Charlie asked.

Edna looked at him quizzically, then thought the detective might be trying a bluff. How could he know that Kevin was the one who broke into Laurel's house.

For a minute, he looked as if he were going to deny the accusation, but then he sighed. "How'd you know it was me? Fingerprints?"

Charlie smiled and nodded. "Since you were in the military, your prints are on file. Pulled you up, nice as you please and just as quick. Even if we didn't have proof of you being in her house, I could have guessed. Her papers were gone, but not the TV or jewelry or anything a burglar usually takes, except maybe for the computer. Don't really have to be a detective to figure it was personal." His smile faded. "So why'd you do it?"

Kevin ran a hand through his dark curls and sighed heavily. "I wanted to find out why she came to Rhode Island, why she wanted to live near my relatives. I was hoping she might have been looking for me, maybe she wanted me back. I loved her, and she loved me … once. That afternoon, I went to the house because I wanted to show her that I've changed." At that, his entire body seemed to sag. "When I heard Miz Davies talking to you that night, I knew it was too late, but I wanted to find something, anything to tell me why she moved here. I wanted time to sort through everything, so I took the lot. It's all in my room at Norm's place."

A loud knocking at the front door sounded like a burst of gunfire in the stillness that followed Kevin's confession. Mary motioned to Edna that she would see who it was and disappeared down the hall. She returned shortly, followed by two uniformed officers.

With a look of panic on his face, Kevin glanced from them to Charlie. "What are they doing here? I told you I didn't kill her." He frowned before his expression turned to one of self-satisfaction. "You can't arrest me for breaking and entering. I'm her next-of-kin, so legally, that night, I entered my own house."

Charlie held up a hand, palm toward Kevin, and slowly shook his head. "As her husband, you're the prime suspect in our murder investigation. I need you to come to the station and answer a few questions. You're not under arrest ..." he paused briefly before adding softly, "not yet."

Chapter 20

"Where have you been?" Edna nearly hissed at Mary, not certain whether to shake her or hug her.

They had collapsed side-by-side onto the sofa while Charlie arranged with the officers to take Kevin to the station where the detective would join them as soon as he'd spoken to Mary. One policeman was instructed to drive Kevin's pickup to the station.

Mary put her gun on the cushion beside her, but before she could turn to Edna, Charlie walked back into the room, distracting them for the moment.

"I'm so glad you showed up when you did," Edna greeted and motioned for him to sit in Albert's chair across the coffee table from the couch. "How did you know not to ring the bell?"

"The black Humvee's out front, the one with the tinted windows that you told me about. When I saw it in your driveway, I thought I'd better let myself in quietly. Since we both thought that car might belong to whoever's been trolling the neighborhood, I thought I'd first better make sure you were okay."

Edna's heart skipped a beat at this news, but before she could react, Mary spoke up.

"Kevin's truck was out there, too," she pointed out. "Did you consider that he might be the dangerous one and not the driver of the Humvee?" Her tone was challenging.

Charlie shook his head. "His behavior's been a little odd, but I figured the bigger threat might come from Edna's other visitor." He leaned forward and rested his elbows on his knees. "In any case, not knowing what to expect, I thought it might be better to apologize after than announce myself too soon."

Edna was still shaken over the image of the huge dark vehicle in her driveway, when Mary spoke again. "It's my car." She looked pleased with herself, as if she'd put one over on the detective. "Actually, it's not really mine. I borrowed it from a friend 'cause I didn't want Kevin to spot me."

"You're the one who nearly drove me off the road?" Edna's relief at seeing her friend alive and well was changing to annoyance that Mary had not only made her worry, but had frightened her half to death with that monster of a vehicle. Curiosity got the best of her. "Why did you keep squirting washer fluid on the windshield?"

Mary's face reddened. "I was trying to flash the lights, so you'd know it was me." In her own defense, she added quickly, "I'm not used to that car. I kept hitting the wrong lever."

The mental image of the looming hulk of a vehicle returned to Edna's mind, along with a fresh picture of Mary behind the wheel, turning on the wipers instead of the headlights. At the image, Edna began to laugh. "I'm not certain I would have guessed it was you even if I'd seen headlights instead of wipers." The release of tension that had gripped her for the last hour was like a dam breaking, and she couldn't control her fit of giggles. As she laughed, first Charlie then a reluctant Mary joined in, until they were clutching their sides with the pain.

When she was finally able to control herself, Edna pulled a tissue out of her pocket and wiped tears from her eyes. "I think Mary needs to explain where she's been for the past two days, but first I could use a drink. Mary, put that gun up somewhere, out of sight. Charlie, build up the fire, if you would. It's gotten cold in here."

Leaving her guests to do her biding, she went to the kitchen for a bottle of wine and two glasses. Knowing Charlie wouldn't drink alcohol before going back to work, she heated a mug of coffee, left over from breakfast. Mary followed her into the kitchen and went through to the mudroom to stow the gun in her down jacket. When she returned to help Edna carry drinks into the other room, she'd also released her hair from the tightly wound scarf and looked more herself.

Once they were resettled comfortably by the blazing fire Charlie had stoked, Edna took a sip of her cabernet and began to feel warmer and more relaxed. Mary and Charlie were now sitting in opposite corners of the sofa across the coffee table from where Edna sat in her favored chair.

Charlie was the first to speak after taking a gulp of coffee and setting the mug on the table. He laid an arm across the back of the couch and half turned to Mary. "I need to get to the station to interview Kevin, but first I want to hear what you have to say. Did you see him enter Laurel Taylor's house, the afternoon she died?"

Mary shook her head. "I went back to the shelter that afternoon to talk to her about Bethany. I drove up toward the garage in case someone else wanted to pull in behind my Jeep. That's when I noticed a man in the back yard. Didn't know it was Kevin at that point. He was crouched, like he was trying to duck out of sight. He was acting so suspicious, I stopped and got out of the car. I pulled out my cell in case I needed to call for help and then moved as quietly as I could, up along the side of the house. I wanted to see what he was doing." Mary paused to stare into her glass, and Edna suspected her friend's mind had drifted to the events of that fateful afternoon.

"Is that when you recognized Kevin?" Charlie prompted.

His voice seemed to bring Mary back to her story, and she raised her head to look at him. "I still didn't know who it was. When I got to the corner of the house and peeked into the yard, he was running toward the back fence. I only saw his back, so I shouted at him. I think I said 'hey' or 'stop' or something like that. He didn't even slow down. I figured I could catch him on the next block, so I ran back to my Jeep. All I could think was to get around to the next street to see who it was."

"That's when he saw you," Edna guessed, remembering the earlier bits of conversation between Kevin and Mary.

She nodded. "I got around the corner and up the side street as fast as I could. There's a four-way stop at the intersection. He was going straight through when I got there. Guess my car must have surprised him 'cause he turned and stared straight at me. I knew he recognized me, but he didn't stop or slow down. That made me wonder what he'd been up to."

"Did you go back to the shelter?" Charlie asked.

She shook her head. "Uh-uh. I took off after him. Wanted to talk to him, find out why he'd been lurking around Laurel's back door. I mean, he acted like he knew he shouldn't be there."

"Why did you disappear?" It was Edna's turn to ask the question uppermost on her mind. "I've been so worried about you. Why didn't you call?"

"First off, I couldn't find my phone. Don't know where I might have left it."

Charlie dropped his arm from the back of the sofa and straightened his left leg. He paused while his hand disappeared into his trouser pocket and reappeared with a cell phone that he handed to her. "Edna found it beside the driveway at CATS. Keep it safe for the next few days, will you? Once this case is closed, you can toss it back into the snow if you'd like." He resumed his half-turned position with a twinkle in his eyes.

Mary grinned, looking slightly embarrassed. "I thought I'd put it back in my jacket pocket when I was running back to the Jeep. Guess not, huh?"

Edna interrupted their exchange, not quite ready to forgive her friend. "You could have called from another phone. It's been two days."

"I didn't want to get you involved. You might've gotten hurt. Besides, if you didn't know where I was, nobody could get it out of you."

Mary's eyes asked forgiveness, but Edna knew her friend's hound-dog personality. Once she caught a scent, Mary was apt to forget about everything else.

"Where did you go? Where have you been all this time?" Edna wasn't going to let Mary off the hook without further explanation.

"I lost Kevin in town when he ran a red light." She looked sideways at Charlie and muttered just loud enough to be understood. "Where are the cops when you need them?"

Charlie snorted a laugh as he slid his hand from the back of the sofa to slap playfully at Mary's shoulder.

"Children," Edna said sternly before smiling affectionately at both of her friends. Her manner sobered as she said, "What about your pets? Where are they?"

"I'm getting to that," Mary said. She took an agonizingly slow sip of her wine. "When I lost Kevin, I was so close to home, I decided not to go back to Laurel's. I had to feed Hank and Spot and get ready for your tree-trimming party." Her smile looked both lopsided and woeful. "It was about an hour later, I found out Laurel was dead."

"How did you hear?" Charlie asked, sitting up.

"Got a call from someone," Mary said.

"Who? Someone at the station? Was it the dispatcher?" he asked.

"You know I don't give up my sources," Mary said, a determined set to her jaw.

"Work that out later," Edna said to Charlie. "I don't care how she found out. I want to know why she disappeared and why she didn't call us."

"I got to thinkin'," Mary said. "Kevin knew I'd seen him at the house. He sure acted weird, but I couldn't say for sure he killed anyone. I didn't get that kind of reading from his actions, but just in case, I thought I'd better play it safe and get lost for a while. If I guessed wrong and he had killed Laurel, he wouldn't stop at doing something to me … or to Hank or Spot." Edna thought she detected a slight catch in Mary's voice when she mentioned her dog and cat. "I wanted to watch him, see what he was up to. If he tried to run, I could tell Charlie where he was. He knows my Jeep, though, so I needed a different car."

"Whose car are you driving? You nearly drove me off the road with that thing, you know." Edna glowered at Mary, but couldn't be angry. Nothing had happened except a momentary fright that she and Gran would end up in a ditch. All "water under the bridge" now.

"Belongs to a friend of mine. Sorry if I scared you, but I'm not used to driving something that big. I did try to flash the headlights, you know."

Before they dissolved into fits of laughter again, Charlie spoke up. "Who's this friend?"

Mary switched her gaze to him before looking down at the wine glass she was twirling between her fingers. "She's a psychologist. Works part-time at the hospital. She and her husband spend Christmas with their daughter in Maine. I look after the house whenever they go away, water her plants and stuff, so I thought it'd be a good place to hide out. Hank and Spot are there now, watching the place, making sure it's safe." She slid her eyes sideways at Charlie, smirked and dodged another playful swipe of his hand.

"What did you find out when you tailed Kevin?" Edna asked to interrupt the horseplay.

"Nothing much," Mary admitted. "The storm hit, so he spent most of the time plowing out driveways. Even did mine and yours, which surprised me. I don't think Norm would approve of his employee spending time on someone who wasn't a payin' customer." She grinned, probably delighted at the thought of the meanest man in town doing anyone an unwitting favor.

"Sounds like he wanted an excuse to hang out in this neighborhood, waiting for you to show up," Charlie said to Mary.

Edna briefly studied the detective. "Do you think he was telling the truth when he said he didn't kill his wife?"

Charlie held up a finger, indicating he'd answer in a minute, before he turned back to Mary. "When you saw him in the backyard at CATS, did you notice if he was wearing gloves?"

She shook her head, but didn't speak, having just taken a sip of wine.

He looked at Edna. "We took prints the afternoon the body was found, before the break-in that night. Next morning, when I saw the place had been ransacked, we got prints again. Unless he was wearing gloves that afternoon, he hadn't been in the house. His prints showed up only in the second set, indicating he was probably our burglar." He turned again to look at Mary with raised eyebrows.

She spoke firmly, sounding confident of her facts. "I'm sure he wasn't wearing gloves. I notice things like that."

"Is it true what he said about breaking into his own house?" Edna asked. "If he's Laurel's heir, you can't charge him with breaking and entering?"

"I let the lawyers work those things out," Charlie said, looking at his watch and getting to his feet. "Mary, I need you to make a statement. I'll let it go for tonight, but I'll expect you at the station around nine tomorrow morning." He motioned to the cell phone she'd laid on the coffee table. "Keep that handy, will you?" Before she could retort, he backed away toward the hall and raised a hand in salute. "If you'll excuse me, ladies, I have to interview a suspect."

Once he was gone, Edna felt drained after the tension of the evening, but she wasn't quite ready to let Mary out of her sight. She asked her to put another log on the fire while she poured them each another half glass of wine. They had just settled back in their chairs when the doorbell rang. They frowned at each other, silently curious as to who would be calling at nine o'clock in the evening, before they both got up and went through to the hall.

Edna opened the door to find Bethany standing on the stoop, hunched into her coat and shivering with cold while falling snow turned the top of her head and shoulders to white.

"I t-t-thought he was never going to l-l-leave," she said through chattering teeth. "C-c-can I come in?"

## Chapter 21

Bethany slipped past them into the house. Before Edna closed the door, she noticed with some dismay that the snow was falling as steadily as ever. Even the lights on the sleigh and reindeer in the middle of the circular driveway wore little caps of snow.

"What are you doing here?" Mary's tone held both surprise and concern.

"L-l-looking for you." Bethany stopped a few feet into the hallway, hugging herself and trembling with cold. She seemed as startled to see Mary as the red-head to see her.

"Did you just drive down from Boston?" Edna was also wondering why the young woman was back in Rhode Island when she'd so recently gone home for the holidays, and in such a rush, too. When Bethany nodded in reply, Edna asked, "How are the roads?" She was thinking about the trains, buses and airplanes, as well, hoping her children would get through from Colorado and not be stranded in some strange and faraway place for Christmas.

"S-s-slow," Bethany looked miserable. "T-t-took me th-th-three hours to g-g-get here."

"You drove down in this weather looking for me?" Mary's brow creased in puzzlement.

"We shouldn't keep her standing in the hall,"

Edna said. "She needs to warm up. Help her off with her coat and take her in by the fire. I'll make some hot chocolate."

"You didn't hitch, did you?" With narrowed eyes, Mary was grilling Bethany when Edna entered the living room carrying a tray with a steaming mug of cocoa, a plate of sugar cookies and another of crackers and cheese.

Bethany shook her head and smiled at Mary who had reseated herself on the couch. "No I didn't hitch. I'm not that crazy. I borrowed my brother's car." Standing with her back to the stoked up fire, Bethany seemed to have warmed up enough that her teeth were no longer chattering. She took the steaming chocolate that Edna handed her and drew it into her chest, clutching the mug with both hands. "Thanks."

"Doesn't his car have a heater?" Mary sounded harsh, almost angry.

Edna sat back in her recliner and mentally began to formulate questions while she waited for Bethany to answer Mary first.

The young woman explained that she'd parked in Mary's driveway, but had pulled in behind the bushes, hoping her car wouldn't be seen from the road. She'd turned off the lights and the engine for the same reason. She hadn't wanted the police to spot her. Once she'd seen them leave, she left the car and walked over to Edna's. She'd been looking for Mary, but when she saw the house was dark and nobody answered the door, Bethany thought Edna would know where Mary was.

"Why didn't you just call me?" Obviously, Mary

had forgotten that nobody had been able to reach her for the past two days.

"I did, but when I called your cell, some guy answered. I hung up." Bethany's eyes widened. "A policeman came to my parents' house, wanting to talk to me. I figured you know the cops, you have friends at the station, so you'd know what I should do. When I couldn't get you on the phone, I had to come see you. I don't want to talk to them alone."

"Why not?" Mary lifted one shoulder as if being interviewed by the police were no big deal, but Edna sensed she was flattered. "You gotta go talk to them. They're not going to leave you alone until you do."

Edna smiled, hoping to reassure Bethany. "Charlie's a good guy. It's part of his investigation into Laurel Taylor's death to question anyone who was at the shelter the day ..." she hesitated before ending faintly, "the day it happened."

"You didn't kill Laurel, did you?"

Even though Mary asked the question as if the thought were ridiculous, Bethany nearly choked on the sip of chocolate she'd just taken. "Of course not."

"Then why are you hiding from the police?" Edna asked in a quieter tone than Mary had used.

"I'm not hiding," Bethany looked at Edna, her jaw set in defiance. "I'll talk to them, but first I want to know what's going on. I thought Mary could tell me what she'd heard from her friends-- you know, what the police found out about how Laurel died and all that. Then, I figured she'd go to the station with me." She gazed at Mary. "When that cop showed up at the house last night, my parents freaked."

"Didn't he question you, the Boston officer?" Edna asked.

"No way," Bethany shook her head emphatically. "I wasn't home. When he told my dad that he wanted to talk to me about a murder, my mother went hysterical. My brother called me at my girlfriend's and told me about it. Said the cop was coming back this morning, and I should probably stay where I was."

Edna was beginning to get annoyed at the young woman's immature attitude and behavior. "If you haven't done anything, why don't you just meet with the police and tell them what you know."

Again, Bethany's mouth set in a stubborn line. "I don't want to be hauled into some police station and grilled for hours." She moved away from the fire and sat on the sofa next to Mary. "I thought if you went with me, they'd be nice and not keep me waiting forever."

Edna swallowed her laughter and shook her head at the misconceptions people get from television shows. Mary did laugh. "That's rubbish. You know better than that."

"Charlie's the one who wants to talk to you, and I've already told you that he's a good person," Edna said, taking a sip of wine before continuing. "He asked a friend of his in Boston to go by your home and ask what you might have seen at CATS the afternoon Laurel died. That's all. He asked his friend a favor, so he wouldn't have to drive up to Boston to see you himself." She leaned toward

Bethany, hoping to impress upon the young woman the importance of any contribution she could make. "He thinks you may have seen something or someone. He only wants a statement from you, as he does from Mary. They're not accusing you of anything. If you did nothing, you have nothing to worry about."

The three women fell silent. Mary picked up a piece of cheese and popped it into her mouth as she turned to look at the fire, now burned down to glowing embers. A minute later, she looked around at Bethany who was leaning over the coffee table to select a cookie. "Tell us about that afternoon. Why did you go to see Laurel, after you sent us to talk to her for you?"

When the young woman seemed not about to answer, Edna prompted, "Vinnie said you saw the Perrys' car in Laurel's driveway. What time was that?"

Bethany shrugged, still studying the plate of cookies. "Three-thirty, four. Somewhere around then."

"Did you go into the house?" Mary asked.

Finally, Bethany sat back on the sofa and looked at Mary with wide eyes. She shook her head vigorously. "No. No way." She relaxed then, but only slightly. "It was probably a good thing someone else was in the house. I had time to think about what I was doing. I don't know why I thought I could stand up to her."

Edna wanted to pin down the vehicle Bethany had seen. "It was definitely the Perrys' car you saw and not their van?" she asked.

"That's right. It was that old Volvo station wagon Roselyn drives."

The image of the mistletoe she'd seen on the floor of the passenger's side formed in Edna's mind. "But you didn't see anyone and you didn't go into Laurel's house?" she asked.

Bethany shook her head again. "No. When I saw that Roselyn was there, I rode around the block a couple of times. By then it was getting really cold. I was thinking about what I'd say to Laurel. Then I realized she'd just kick me out of the house like she did before." She scowled. "It just wasn't worth it."

"Are you certain it was Roselyn in the house?" Edna asked.

Bethany shrugged and took a bite of cookie. "I didn't actually see her, but I'm sure it was her Volvo."

"Did you see anyone else in the neighborhood when you were riding around?" Mary asked.

"There was a guy installing a cable TV dish on someone's house down the block, and a Honeydew Home Repairs truck on the next street over. That was sort of weird. The truck wasn't parked in front of any house or anything. It didn't look like he was working. He was just sitting there. I saw him staring at me when I rode up the street toward him. I crossed over so I wouldn't pass close to his truck. I think he's another reason I decided to head back to town. He scared me a little, just sitting there and staring."

Mary nodded at Edna. "Must've been not long before I got there." Then she frowned. "I didn't see the Perrys' car, though. I think you're right that it must have been Roselyn, but I didn't see her if she went back toward town when she left. We would have passed each other, I'm sure."

Edna thought they'd exhausted all that Bethany knew about the afternoon at the cat shelter. The talk about bicycles, though, made Edna remember Charlie's mysterious rider. "Did you bike out to this neighborhood the other evening? It would have been the night after we met in Mary's kitchen?" she said to Bethany.

"Eew. No way I'd ride a bike way out here in the dark." She hugged herself and settled back in the corner of the sofa as she frowned at Edna. "Why?"

Edna explained about Charlie's bicycle thief and the tracks he'd seen in the snow the morning he came to help hang Christmas lights around the house and the yew trees.

Bethany laughed, seeming to enjoy a private joke. "That must have been Codfish. He told me this story about how he was in town one night after lending me Vinnie's bike. He was walking around town, killing time, when he spotted this bike leaning against a building. He said the temptation was too much. He hopped on and rode up and down a few side streets. He probably didn't remember exactly where the bike had been by the time he finished with it." This time when she chuckled, Mary and Edna joined her. "He said he did that a couple of times, mainly just practicing. I gave him his bike back the afternoon I left Mary's. Went right to the Kitchen and left it behind the diner so he could put it in his truck."

"Do you think he would have peddled all the

way out here?" Edna asked, still amused at the story and thinking Charlie would be, too.

Bethany nodded and smiled mischievously. "I betcha anything he was checking on Miz Cravendorf. He's got a thing for her, you know. He heard her granddaughter was going to be out of town for a few days, and he wanted to make sure she was okay. His truck makes one heck of a noise, so I bet he rode the bike so she wouldn't know he was watching out for her. Guess the snow put a stop to that."

"Or he decided the two-mile trip was harder than he thought, particularly in the cold." Mary laughed.

"That would explain the footprints on the deck, too," Edna said, and told them the rest of what she and Charlie had seen, but not what she and the detective had speculated.

The women all fell silent again, each lost in her own thoughts for a minute or two as they stared at the dying embers in the hearth. Edna remembered how she and Charlie had worried about someone lurking around the neighborhood. That thought led her to wonder about Kevin and his odd behavior. "Do you think Kevin might have pushed Laurel down the stairs?" she asked Mary, breaking the silence.

Mary shook her head. "If he was going to kill someone, it would have been Jake. You saw the way Laurel threw herself at our handsome young vet. If Kevin had seen that, he'd 've been jealous as all get-out."

Edna thought again of the crumpled mistletoe on the floor of the Perrys' Volvo. Maybe Kevin wasn't the only jealous one. She told Mary and Bethany what she had seen through the car window. "Do you think Roselyn could have killed Laurel? Or, at least if she was at CATS that afternoon, maybe she saw something. Maybe Laurel was already dead by the time Roselyn got to the shelter."

Bethany shivered, but not from the cold this time. "You mean Laurel might have been getting murdered right when I was there?"

"Of course not. Roselyn wouldn't't've done a thing like that." Mary shook her and turned to Edna. "We could go ask her what she saw, though. She's at the clinic every morning to feed the animals in the back kennel. We can go see her first, then go to the grocery store before half the town is up. That Humvee is great in the snow. If it gets much deeper, you won't be able to budge that Buick of yours."

"Tomorrow is Christmas Eve. Won't the clinic be closed?" Edna asked. She'd be glad for the lift to Stop and Shop, but wasn't sure about wasting precious time to satisfy Mary's obsession over criminal matters.

Mary set her empty goblet on the coffee table. "Doesn't matter if they're closed or not. She still has to go in to tend to the animals. Whadda ya say? I'll pick you up at eight." She grinned. "You'll like riding in the Humvee. I'm thinking of getting one."

"You two can get up early, but I'm sleeping in." Bethany pushed herself to her feet. "After you finish talking to Roselyn and buying groceries, will you go to the police station with me?" she asked Mary.

"What about your party? It's tomorrow night,

and you're expecting quite a crowd," Edna said, thinking of her own last-minute chores.

Mary shrugged and stood up. "If this storm continues, half the people won't show up for my party. Besides, we already did the baking. Priscilla and Faye are catering the rest of the food. We'll have time to go ask Roselyn a few questions in the morning. It won't take long." She glanced up at the grandfather clock in a corner of the room. "Right now, Hank and Spot are probably worried about me. Come on, Bethany. My friend's house has an extra room you can use. I'll drive you to your brother's car, and you can follow me. That way, I'll know where you are, and we can both go talk to Charlie tomorrow."

Edna saw them out, noticing with alarm the several new inches of snow in her driveway as Mary drove off in the Humvee. Returning to the living room, she banked the fire and took the dishes into the kitchen. She stacked them in the sink to wash in the morning. Tiredly, she switched off the downstairs lights and headed for the stairs. As she passed her small office, she glanced in at the boxes of cards still yet to be written and addressed. The cards and the last-minute grocery shopping were all that were left on her to-do list. As if she could make this particular chore go away, she shut the door to her office and wearily climbed the stairs to bed.

## Chapter 22

As promised, Mary pulled up to the house at eight the following morning. Another six inches of snow had accumulated during the night, but now the sky was cloudless. Dawn had broken and the world looked like a winter wonderland. Climbing up into the passenger's seat of the Humvee, Edna asked Mary, "Do you know if the airports are open?"

Mary shrugged as she put the car in gear and drove slowly around the circle to the road. "Don't know." She slid her eyes to look briefly at Edna. "Haven't you heard from Starling or Grant? Won't they call to let you know when they're flying in?"

Edna shook her head, feeling a heavy sadness in her chest. "I've been trying to reach them, but they don't answer their phones. I hope that means they're in the air, heading this way, and not sitting on a runway somewhere."

"They'll be okay. Don't worry. They'll get here," Mary said, sounding more confident than Edna felt.

Perry's Animal Clinic looked deserted when they pulled into the parking lot, but Mary seemed to know where she was going. Following fresh car tracks, she drove around to a smaller lot in the rear. A series of dog runs made of chain link fencing occupied most of the area behind the building's extension. The old Volvo stood in front of a back door leading to the kennels.

Mary parked on the far side of the wagon and, as Edna got out of the Humvee, she noticed the back of the Perrys' car was filled with boxes and suitcases. *They must be taking quite a long holiday vacation*, she thought as she trudged after Mary.

Inside, the boarding room smelled faintly of disinfectant and slightly stronger of wet fur. Roselyn was crouched before a waist-high counter at the far end of the room, apparently having just finished securing a bandage to the foreleg of a German Shepherd. Extra strips of surgical tape dripped from the counter's edge.

Edna and Mary stood silently and watched as the veterinarian's wife stood, tossed a roll of tape and scissors onto the shelf, and drew forward two stainless steel dog dishes. Either she hadn't heard them enter or she was ignoring them while she scooped dry food from a large bag into the bowls. The Shepherd sat patiently, watching the process. In one of the six cages lining the far wall, a Boxer stood at attention, wagging her stub of a tail. Both dogs were so completely absorbed in waiting for Roselyn to give them their breakfasts, they gave only a perfunctory glance toward the newcomers.

Edna was reminded of her children when they were small and used to watch very carefully while she prepared plates of food. Once she tired of their arguing over who had received a grain more than another, she turned the task over to them. Whoever divvied up the portions received the last dish after everyone else had chosen.

With her eye on the canine and his on the dishes of kibbles, Roselyn walked over to an open pen and placed one of the bowls inside. When the Shepherd began to eat, she closed the door and turned to deliver the second dish to the Boxer.

As Edna waited for Roselyn to acknowledge them, she found herself looking into the yellow eyes of a short-haired tabby close to her shoulder. Stretched along the back wall were a series of two-story cat apartments. Each held a litter box on the bottom floor and a ramp to the upper story. The top level contained a bed and a shelf where the cats could sit and look out onto the back parking lot and dog runs. In warmer weather, the trees beyond the lot would attract a variety of birds for the cats' entertainment, as well, Edna noticed. She saw the three felines from Laurel's shelter huddled together, two pens down from the short-hair next to her.

The center aisle was free of obstruction and wide enough for two adults to walk side-by-side. Cupboards above the counter made up the narrow, far wall. More cupboards had been built in below the workspace at both ends, and a backless barstool occupied the kneehole in the middle.

Completing her tasks, Roselyn finally looked toward her visitors with a questioning frown.

"Hi, Roz," Mary called out as she walked down the length of the room.

"What are you doing here?" Roselyn asked in her quiet voice, without returning a greeting. "The clinic is closed." She leaned back against the counter and folded her arms across her chest.

"That's okay." Mary moved to stand next to her.

"We came to see you."

Edna stopped a few feet short of the other women. Letting Mary do the talking, she observed Roselyn Perry and noticed something she'd never been close enough to see before. A small vertical scar was faintly visible on her upper lip. Edna wondered how old Roselyn had been when surgery had been performed, and if a cleft lip were at least part of the reason for the woman's shyness. She also noticed that Roselyn's eyes were red-rimmed and dark shadows beneath spoke of sleeplessness.

"Me? Why do you want to see me?" Her reply was quiet and unconvincing, as if she knew the answer. She studied Mary with suspicion, but didn't hold the gaze. Instead, she turned away to watch the Shepherd as he finished his breakfast and searched the floor for any bits that might have escaped his bowl.

"Laurel Taylor," was Mary's reply. Her air was casual, but Edna knew her neighbor would be aware of any twitch in Roselyn's face.

The younger woman's scowl deepened. "What about her?"

"Someone saw your car in her driveway the afternoon she died."

Mary shrugged as if it were no big deal, but Roselyn remained wary as she pushed herself up and half-turned to straighten items on the counter. She picked up the roll of white tape and the scissors and began to cut long strips, adding them to the row already hanging from the edge of the counter. Strange, thought Edna, but perhaps it was something to concentrate on instead of her visitors' faces. Was it shyness or guilt that made her act so guarded?

"I was here that afternoon." Roselyn's voice was so soft, Edna had to strain to understand her words.

"Was it Laurel's mistletoe in your car?" Edna asked, hoping to shake the woman out of her quiet passiveness.

Roselyn's eyes shifted quickly to Edna's face and then to Mary's before returning to the scissors in her hand. "I don't like your questions. Please leave. I have work to do."

At that moment, Edna sensed someone behind her and spun around as Jake strode up.

"What's going on? What are you ladies doing back here?" His tone held only curiosity.

Hearing a yelp of protest, Edna swung back again, stunned by what she saw. Roselyn had hold of Mary's arms just above the elbows. Mary's hands were behind her back and a length of tape bound her wrists together. Before Edna fully understood what was happening, she felt Jake's strong hands clasp her upper arms.

"What are you doing? Let me go," she cried, suddenly afraid.

As she spoke, Jake's voice rose above hers. "You jumped the gun a bit, Roz. What are you thinking?"

"They would have stopped us." Previously so meek, Roselyn now seemed to be the one in control.

"I could have gotten rid of them without this unnecessary complication." Jake spoke reasonably, but sighed with resignation. "Now, we have no choice."

"They would have called the police." Roselyn seemed to withdraw again when she had her husband's cooperation. She had made the first move, but he was taking charge.

Edna had stopped struggling against Jake's grip while husband and wife talked. She saw Mary had done the same, as if the Perrys had made some ridiculous mistake and would let their captives go. The situation changed at Jake's next words and both hostages began to twist and wriggle to free themselves.

"Strap her wrists," he said, nodding toward Mary.

At once, Roselyn smashed her knee into the back of Mary's knee, causing the leg to buckle, and Mary was instantly on the floor.

Both prisoners protested loudly and thrashed against their assailants as their wrists and ankles were bound. Edna was only vaguely aware that the dogs were restless and whining while the cats watched in silence.

"What do you think you're doing?" she asked, feeling her face flush with anger. She was sitting on the floor, knees raised while Jake strapped her calf-high boots together just above the ankles. Roselyn, apparently having secured Mary to her satisfaction, was pulling tape off the counter to wrap Edna's wrists more securely than the single strip Jake had used.

"You don't have to tie us up," Mary said drolly as she writhed on the floor beside Edna. "We'll leave quietly, if that's what you want."

Edna wondered how Roselyn could have gotten

control of the larger Mary, but soon realized that the veterinarian's wife was used to grappling with large animals and was probably every bit as strong as Mary, besides being twenty years younger.

The tighter her bonds got, the more Edna's temper rose. She didn't share Mary's ill-timed humor. Staring fixedly at the top of Jake's head as he bent to his task, she said, "Obviously, one or both of you had something to do with Laurel Taylor's death." Without waiting for him to confirm or deny the accusation, she went on. "You'll never get away with it, and you're making things worse by tying us up."

Jake finally looked up at her as he handed the roll of tape and scissors to his wife. He seemed sad and resigned. "I'm really sorry," he said. "I didn't plan things to happen this way. I didn't plan anything to happen the way it has." He ran a hand over his chin, glancing up and far away. "You shouldn't have come here. Ten more minutes and we'd have been gone."

"You won't get far, you know," Mary sputtered, now sounding equally as angry as Edna felt. "Go to the police and confess. Things'll go better for you."

As if snapped out of a trance, Jake stood, a grim expression hardening his features as he looked down at them. "Laurel's death was an accident, but who's to believe me with no witnesses. I can't go to jail. I'd never make it in prison, and Roselyn won't make it on her own. I'm all she's got."

As he said this, Roselyn came forward and stepped briefly into his arms. She rested her forehead against his chest for a second or two before moving away toward the back door. She hadn't spoken and she didn't look back. Jake stared at Edna for another heartbeat before turning to follow his wife.

Mary, lying on her side next to Edna, was watching them retreat, too. "You can't leave us here like this," she called.

"Nobody will find us until after Christmas," Edna added, her voice trailing off as the horror of that thought struck home.

Roselyn disappeared out to the parking lot without the slightest hesitation, but Jake stood and looked back. When he hesitated, Edna's heart lifted with hope until he spoke. "Juliana will come in tonight to feed the animals. She'll cut you free. By then, we should be far enough away. I'm really sorry we had to do this. If you just hadn't come here this morning …" He didn't finish the sentence. Instead, shaking his head, he slipped out after his wife and shut the door.

Edna heard the sound of a keyed bolt sliding into place, followed soon by a car's engine and then silence. She looked over at Mary. "We're in it this time."

Chapter 23

"Don't worry," Mary said, struggling to sit up. "Bethany knows where we are."

"Bethany is sleeping in," Edna reminded her. "When she wakes up and you haven't come home, she'll think either we're still shopping or you're at my house and will be home soon." At least a full half-minute of silence passed before Edna said in a quieter voice, "How long do you think it will take her to realize something's wrong?"

As she spoke, Edna began shifting her legs in a sideways crab-walk to turn herself around so she could examine the wall and space behind her. The manoeuver wasn't difficult since her coat slid easily on the linoleum floor while the rubber heels of her boots held firm. With her back to the room, she was sitting knee to shoulder with Mary and about two feet away.

"Mary, look," she said, pointing with her chin to a wall phone in the recess above the counter. A long, curled cord connected the receiver to the cradle. "If I could stand, I can dislodge that phone and dial nine-one-one."

"How're you gonna do that?"

"With my nose."

Mary snorted. "Not 'dial.' I meant how're you gonna stand up with your feet taped together?"

"I attended enough of my children's gymnastic events to figure it out, I think. Use your heels to push yourself over to that cupboard. I'm going to back up against it. If I can brace my knees against your back, I think I can use the tension to help me stand. Just keep pushing back against my legs."

Hope and excitement filled her chest, as Edna inched her way over to the wall. She positioned herself so that, as she slid up the wall, she would avoid both the hinges and the handle of the cupboard door. Mary, following Edna's example, propelled her way backwards until her shoulders were against Edna's drawn-up knees. Edna shimmied against the smooth cupboard door and, with the help of her hands pressing into the wood, managed to raise herself three or four inches off the floor. She was momentarily stymied when her boots wouldn't slide backwards under Mary's pressure.

"Hold on," she said.

"What's wrong?" Mary tried to look around, but couldn't crane her neck far enough.

"My feet need to move closer to the wall as I go up. Let me think."

Edna sat for a minute before deciding the best thing to do would be to pull her legs into her chest as far as she could manage. She'd still be slanted, balancing on her head and shoulder blades, but she might be able to propel herself upright without falling over on Mary. She explained what she wanted to do and, to her delight and surprise, it worked. The final thrust was somewhat awkward when she nearly fell before pressing her knees into Mary's shoulders to balance herself, but she was standing.

"Don't move for a minute," she said. "I need to catch my breath."

By the time she'd rested for nearly a minute, Edna had figured out how she would manoeuver the next foot to the rim of the counter. With her ankles bound, she'd definitely fall over, if she tried to hop. Her legs had been outstretched when Jake bound her ankles, so one boot sole was a fraction higher than the other. She found, however, with her right foot flat on the floor, she could press down with either toe or heel of her left foot to help her balance. Shifting both feet together in a careful toe-then-heel movement, she first backed up against the wall where she could use her hands to help steady herself, and then slowly sidled her way to the counter. When she was able to grasp the lip of the shelf, she looked back down at Mary and saw her friend grinning up at her.

"Nice goin', Edna."

Pleased and encouraged, she twisted her body slightly to study the phone while she maintained a tentative grip on the counter. The bottom of the receiver was about even with her temple. Straining her neck, she was able to nudge the receiver up with her chin. Loosened from its cradle, the instrument hit the side of her face, slid down to bounce off the counter and landed with a crash on the floor. Edna stood still, her heart in her throat.

Mary fell on her side and snaked her way over to put an ear to the receiver.

"Is it broken?" Edna asked, barely daring to breath.

"Maybe. I don't hear a dial tone."

Edna stretched her neck again until her nose pressed against the nine on the keypad. Standing on her tiptoes, she was just able to hit the one. Pushing against the button twice, she carefully lowered herself from her toes and looked down at Mary. "Anything?" she asked in a near whisper.

Mary shook her head. "Maybe this one's connected to the phone at the front desk and you can't call out from here."

Edna glanced at the cradle. "I don't think so. It looks like a regular phone, not an intercom."

Mary sighed. "Well, maybe there's a some sort of number or code you need to know to get a dial tone."

As they talked, Edna began to look around for any other means of freeing them from the tape. There were a few plastic bottles and small tubs on the counter, a tube of some sort of medication, a drinking glass and … she spotted the tape and scissors. Roselyn had thrown them to the back of the three-foot-deep counter.

Edna carefully twisted her body, regretful of having to let go of the counter with her hands, and half-fell onto the shelf. Pushing and wriggling, raising herself on her toes, no matter what she tried, she could not reach the scissors with her head. In her overcoat, she was hot and exhausted when she finally gave up. She was resting on the shelf, trying to decide what to do next, when she heard a muffled ringing.

"What's that?" She slid around to look down at Mary.

"It's my cell phone," Mary said, sounding surprised and excited. She rolled over and was struggling to sit up when the ringing stopped. "Bet that's Charlie. I was supposed to be at the station at nine. It must be well past that by now."

Edna rolled over and tried to grasp the lip again. Either she turned too fast or her hands were numb, but she couldn't find the edge and began to slip off. Turning her body as she fell, she managed to land on her hip and shoulder instead of her face. She lay still for half a minute, taking mental inventory of any pain before she opened her eyes to look at Mary.

"You okay?" Her friend's eyes were wide with worry.

"I'm fine. Just a bit shaken. My coat padded the fall." As she spoke, Edna's mind swung to what she'd heard. She couldn't help sounding accusatory when she demanded, "Why didn't you tell me you had your phone with you?"

"I didn't remember it was in my pocket. I've been just a little distracted." Mary sounded annoyed and petulant when she added, "Where's your phone?"

"In my tote."

"Where's your tote?"

"In your car."

"So *fine*. Don't blame me." Mary's voice was filled with frustration and resentment.

Edna felt ashamed of her implied criticism. "Let's not quarrel. If I back up to you, I can get the phone out of your pocket. You'll have to guide your jacket to my hands."

As she spoke, she rolled onto her other side and, with Mary's help, fumbled for the mobile and pulled it free. Lying on the floor with the phone held in her bound hands, she flicked up the lid and ran her fingers across the surface. Her momentary elation dissolved into despair. "It feels almost smooth. I'm not certain I can distinguish the different buttons. How do I turn it on? What do I push if it starts to ring again?"

"Hold on," Mary commanded. "I can't see what you're doing. Your hand's in the way."

"I can't put my finger on a button without my hand there."

Both women were snapping at each other, and Edna's nerves were beginning to fray when she heard another voice. "What's going on here?"

All the frustration, fear and anger she'd felt that morning burbled into her throat and threatened to come out as a howl as she spun her body around to see Charlie practically running down the length of the room. He bent to look into the face of each woman, asking, "Are you okay? Anyone hurt?"

"Scissors," Edna squeaked out through her tight throat. "On the counter."

Instead of heeding her, he reached into his pants pocket and came out with a jackknife. With deft but careful strokes, he sliced through the tape between Edna's wrists and then between her boots, leaving her to unwrap herself while he turned to Mary.

"I told you to keep your phone handy, didn't I," he quipped, as he cut her bonds.

"It was right here at my side," she joked back, rubbing her wrists after removing the tape.

On his knees, Charlie turned back to help Edna remove the last of the tape from her boots. Impulsively, she reached out and hugged him.

"I've never been so happy to see anyone in my whole life."

Once she'd released him, he helped her to stand. She rested against the counter while he gave Mary a hand up. Finally able to remove their coats, the women both began to walk tentatively and swing their arms to get circulation flowing again.

As soon as Edna began to feel better, she went to Mary and put her arms around her friend in a gentle hug. "I'm sorry I was cross with you. Please forgive me."

Mary returned the hug. "Guess we were both a little cranky. Good thing Charlie showed up when he did." She stood back and smiled down at Edna. "I'll forgive you, if you forgive me."

Feeling greatly relieved, Edna smiled back. "Done," she said before turning to Charlie. "How did you know where to find us?"

"Jake Perry told me," Charlie said. "And he pointed me to where I could find the spare key to the back door."

"And here I thought you'd traced me through the GPS on my cell phone--*which*," Mary reminded him again, "was right here at my side."

"I would have, if I'd been sure you hadn't left it on Edna's coffee table," he chided her before growing serious again.

"You said Jake told you where to find us?" Edna interrupted their banter, wondering at Charlie's news.

"That's right. I was in the office waiting for a certain someone to show up for her interview ..." At this, he scowled good-naturedly at Mary. "And while I was waiting, I happened to be talking to our dispatcher when the call came in about the Perrys. Seems Doctor Perry was driving too fast and skidded off the road on Route One, down near Charlestown. Because his wife wasn't wearing her seat belt, she was thrown against the dashboard. Jake called nine-one-one for an ambulance, but the squad car got there first. Apparently, he was feeling guilty about leaving you two here, so he alerted the cop who radioed in to us."

Ignoring his teasing jibes, Mary said, "Did you arrest him?"

"Do you want to press charges?" Charlie's smile vanished as he became serious again.

"Dunno," she said. "But you should arrest him for the murder of Laurel Taylor. He all but admitted he ..." She hesitated for a beat. "or she ... one of the Perrys killed Laurel," she ended lamely, her voice fading along with her certainty.

"Exactly." Charlie picked up on her indecision. "So far, we have no proof that either of the Perrys killed Laurel Taylor."

"If they're not in jail, where are they?" Edna asked.

"The EMT's took her to the hospital. At the least, she's suffered a concussion. Jake's with her. I'm going over there next to talk to him."

"What time is it?" Mary suddenly seemed anxious.

"Nearly noon," Charlie said.

She pulled her jacket off the counter. "Priscilla and Faye will be at my house in another couple of hours with food for the party, and I need to get to the grocery store. Comin', Edna?"

Edna shook her head. "I'd like to go with Charlie to see Jake and Roselyn." She turned to him with a raised eyebrow. "If that's okay."

He nodded. "I'm not conducting an official interview at this point, so I don't see why not."

Mary shrugged into her parka. "Suit yourself. Anything I can get you from the market?"

Edna mentally reviewed the items she needed. "Maybe a half gallon of milk. I can get by for the next couple of days with what's in the larder. My family will just have to 'make do or do without'," she quoted her grandmother who had lived through the Great Depression.

"I'll see she gets home," Charlie said before turning to Edna. "What time is Starling flying in? When I spoke to her last night, she said their plane was due to land in Providence at one o'clock. With all the cancellations yesterday, I'm thinking there's a good chance their flight has been changed, and I don't want to leave you alone until someone can be with you."

"I wasn't able to reach either Starling or Grant this morning. I'm hoping it's because they were in the air with their phones turned off," Edna said. She didn't want to think about her children not showing up that afternoon, so she said nothing more.

Mary's concentration seemed wholly on zipping her jacket and pulling on her gloves. She looked up only when the other two fell silent. "Okay. I'm off then. See you later." She waved and headed for the back door.

*She's up to something*, Edna thought, but didn't have time to dwell on what it might be before Charlie pressed his hand to the middle of her back, indicating they should follow Mary outside.

"My tote," Edna called, as she saw the Humvee skidding across the snow-packed parking lot toward the exit.

"This it?" Charlie held up a colorful cloth bag that had been resting on the hood of his unmarked vehicle.

She sighed with relief, grateful to Mary for being so thoughtful. Quickly, she pulled open the side pocket where she kept her mobile, hoping to see she'd received a message from one of her children. When she found the pocket empty, she frantically rummaged through the items inside. Finally looking up in despair to see no sign of Mary, she wailed to Charlie, "My phone must have dropped out in her car."

Chapter 24

At the hospital, Edna and Charlie found Jake Perry sitting at his wife's bedside. In the private room, Roselyn was resting back against three pillows. A lump the size of a small egg at her hairline was mottled red and black. Husband and wife were holding hands, looking unhappy and uncertain even before they noticed the two visitors enter the room.

Jake's face flushed when he saw Edna. Half rising, he said, "Are you okay?"

She went to the foot of the bed and gripped the rail. She had mixed feelings about this couple whom she'd genuinely liked, but who'd tied her up so dispassionately. Not knowing what to say, she merely nodded as Jake sank back in his chair.

Charlie walked over to stand beside the bed, across from Jake. "How're you feeling," he said looking down at Roselyn.

She murmured something Edna couldn't make out. It was obvious that the woman wasn't "fine" though.

"Tell me about Laurel Taylor." Charlie could have been speaking to either one of the Perrys as he pulled a chair closer to the bed and sat. Another chair stood in a corner of the room where Edna could sit, if she chose. She respected the fact that the detective was working and left her to take care of herself.

"Not much to tell, really," Jake said, taking his wife's left hand in both of his. He played with her gold wedding band instead of looking at the detective.

"I think there is," Charlie said. He shrugged out of his topcoat and let it fall back over the chair. "Why don't we start with your visit to the cat shelter on the day she died? You were both at the house, at one time or another. That right?"

Roselyn had turned to face her husband and the window beyond. She was watching Jake's face now with an expression of love and trust, apparently leaving the story-telling up to him.

He nodded once at Edna before looking across the bed at Charlie. "She saw me arrive with Norm Wilkins that morning. We were there to take photographs for Laurel to use to promote her shelter. I enjoy taking pictures of animals. It's a hobby of mine, so I don't mind doing it for other folks."

Listening to his inconsequential ramblings, Edna sensed the vet's reluctance to get to the point. Charlie must have, too, because he prompted, "So you set up to take some pictures. I understand Norm posed as Santa for you."

"That's right. We spent about an hour, maybe a little more. Roselyn arrived as we were packing up to leave. She usually checked on the cats a couple times a week, trimmed their claws, brushed their teeth. Whatever was needed."

"What was Laurel doing while you were taking

pictures?" Charlie asked.

"She was right in the middle of everything. Insisted on posing in several of the photos. Sat on Norm's lap for some."

"She was acting like a silly teenager, for heaven's sake--as if she was a cute, young cheerleader." Roselyn's soft but angry voice surprised them all. She twisted around to scowl at Charlie. "I went there to check on the cats and watch some of the picture-taking. I had just come in the front door when I heard Jake tell Norm they were finished, so I went straight through to put my bag in the kitchen. By the time I got back, Norm was headed out to the van with the tripod and props. I went into the front room to see Laurel tiptoeing up behind my husband, holding some mistletoe up in the air. His camera case was on the card table and he was bent over, packing his gear away while she was sneaking up behind him." At this, Roselyn gave a self-satisfied nod, but still looked angry. "I stopped her before she could kiss him."

If Charlie were surprised at Roselyn's willingness to speak, he didn't show it. "How did you do that?" he asked.. "How did you stop her?"

"I grabbed her shoulder and pulled her away from him."

"Was that all? You just pulled her away?"

Roselyn shook her head. "That was all I intended to do--just get her off my husband--but she laughed. She started waving the mistletoe over her head, sashaying around, making fun of me. When I tried to grab it, she moved her arm back." Roselyn looked down at her hands and paused briefly. She stopped frowning and gazed matter-of-factly at Charlie. "So I slapped her. Hard. Across the face."

"Honey," Jake spoke, interrupting her. "You don't have to say anymore. You had nothing to do with …"

She turned and held her fingers to his lips. "I want to tell him. It'll be okay." She waited for her husband to say something, but he only nodded and kissed her fingers before she drew her hand away.

Edna was spellbound both by the tale Roselyn told and by the loving interaction between husband and wife.

Rolling her head back toward Charlie, Roselyn continued her story, smiling faintly, but with no joy. "I didn't like hitting her, but it worked. She brought her arm down, and I grabbed the mistletoe. That's when Jake stepped between us. As far as I was concerned, that was the end of it. Laurel sat on a chair, holding a hand to her cheek and pretending to cry. We left her there." Roselyn picked at the hem of the sheet that covered her to her chest. "I told Jake to go on to the van, and I'd be out in a minute. I had to get my tote from the kitchen. When I saw the teapot on the table, I didn't think twice. It was a good place to get rid of the mistletoe. I sure didn't want it. After that, I took my bag and left. I was still pretty mad when I got to the front door, so I reached up and pulled the rest of the mistletoe off the light. I was going to drop it on the lawn, but I figured she'd just hang it back up again, so I tossed it into the car."

"Do you know mistletoe is poisonous?" Edna asked. She knew she shouldn't interrupt Charlie's interview, but she was curious. The words had come out before she could stop them.

Roselyn's eyes grew wide. "No." The word came out in a startled gasp as she shook her head. The action must have caused some pain because she winced, sagged back onto the pillows and closed her eyes. Her long speech was over.

The image of the crushed mistletoe entwined with a red ribbon popped into Edna's head as Charlie's gaze left Roselyn and turned to Jake. "Your Volvo was seen in the driveway later that day. Which of you went back?"

"Me," Jake said. "I went back about four o'clock."

Edna noticed Roselyn's hand tighten over her husband's as if for support and reassurance.

He continued to speak to Charlie as if he hadn't felt his wife's grip, although his eyes flicked to hers for an instant. "After my last patient, I was going to download the pictures I'd taken. When I opened my case, I noticed one of the cameras was missing. I suspect Laurel took it, knowing I'd come for it. When I got to CATS, she was a little unsteady on her feet, as if she'd had a drink or two, although I didn't smell liquor on her breath." He brushed a hand over his mouth and chin and studiously avoided looking at his wife.

"I don't know. She might have had some of the tea from the pot. Her words were slurred, too, but only slightly, not really enough for me to think she was about to pass out or anything. She asked me, since I was there, if I would change a light bulb for her. The one at the top of the stairs had burned out."

At this, he paused and looked at Charlie with a sheepish expression. "Old trick, right?"

Charlie bobbed his head and gave a half-smile of sympathy, but said nothing.

Jake went on. "She said the new bulbs were in the upstairs hall closet, but that was an excuse for her to follow me without my being suspicious of her intentions. When I turned my back and reached up to unscrew the burned-out bulb, I felt her arms go around my chest and her head press against my back. She took me completely by surprise. I grabbed hold of her wrists, loosened her grip and twisted around to face her. I told her to lay off, that I wasn't interested."

He rubbed the back of his wife's hand in a nervous gesture. Relating what had happened, rousing memories that he'd probably wanted to bury forever, he stopped talking and bowed his head.

Charlie finally broke the growing silence. "Go on."

Jake shrugged and met Charlie's eyes. "She reached for me again. Actually, it was more like she was falling toward me, but I was ready for her by then. I held onto her upper arms and gave her a good shake to let her know I meant business. When I let go, she stumbled backwards and tripped over her own feet. I didn't push her. Honest." His eyes seemed to plead for Charlie to understand. "She was so close to the top of the staircase, she just backed off into air and fell. As soon as I realized what was happening, I tried to grab her, but I missed. When I got to the bottom of the steps, I could tell her neck had been broken. There was nothing I could do to save her."

"Why didn't you call an ambulance or the police?" Charlie asked.

Edna was impressed with the detective's cool demeanor. Her heart was racing with the images Jake's story had invoked, and she realized she'd brought a hand up to her mouth. She knew Charlie to be sensitive enough to be moved by Jake's confession, but he didn't show it.

At the moment, Jake was shaking his head. "I don't know why. If I could turn the clock back, do everything differently, I would. What can I say? I panicked and did a stupid thing."

Edna heard a slight noise over her shoulder and spun to see a man and woman standing in the doorway. They both wore police uniforms. The man had on a navy blue parka. The woman's overcoat was draped over one arm.

Charlie nodded at them, before turning back to Jake. "Officer Hanley will drive you to the station and take your statement. Officer Franklin," he nodded at the woman, "will stay here with your wife. We'll need her to make a statement, too, but it can wait until the doctor releases her."

As the officers moved into the room, following his orders, Charlie stood and held a hand out to Edna. "Come. I'll take you home now."

## Chapter 25

"What will happen to the Perrys?" Edna asked Charlie when they were in his car and on their way to her house.

He glanced her way before returning his attention to the road. The sun was bright, the day was warming up, and the snow on the roads was turning to a slippery, wet mush. He answered her with a question of his own. "Will you or Mary be filing a complaint?"

"I won't. I doubt if Mary will. I think they have enough to contend with, and Jake did tell you where to find us." She leaned her head back. Charlie's sedan was not the most comfortable car, but at the moment, the seat felt soft and almost luxurious under her aching body.

"Then the charges will be specific to Laurel Taylor's death--leaving the scene and failure to report, among others. The lawyers take over from here. I've done my job, now I'm out of it." Changing the subject, he said, "How are you feeling?"

She gave him a weary smile. "I'm pretty certain I can imagine what a beating with a rubber hose would feel like."

He chuckled. "You're almost home. If you want to lie down for a while, I'll make you a cup of tea.

Course, it won't taste as good as yours."

She managed a weak laugh, feeling the sound vibrate in every sore muscle. "The first thing I'm going to do is take a nice hot bath. After that, I may take you up on the offer." She rolled her head in his direction. "But you must have work to do. Shouldn't you go to the station?"

His eyes met hers for an instant. "I have a few cleanup chores, but they can wait. I don't want to leave you until someone else is in the house."

His words caused a lump to form in her throat when she remembered that nobody would be home to greet her at the door. She was certain it was exhaustion from her morning's ordeal that was making her feel sorry for herself. And, of course, Benjamin would rush to meet her. The thought relieved some of the tightness in her throat. When she could speak, she said, "I won't see Albert until Mary's party this afternoon, and goodness knows when Starling and Grant will arrive, even if they did manage to get on a plane today." Her weariness was undermining her usual optimism, but at the moment, she wasn't strong enough to fight it.

They both fell silent until Charlie turned into the Davieses' property and parked behind the Kia which stood behind Edna's Buick. Both vehicles were blanketed with several inches of snow, as was the driveway. He helped Edna around the brick path to the mudroom door. "You go get your hot bath, and if you hand me that shovel, I'll do the walks while I still have my boots on."

Edna spent the next half hour luxuriating in a bubble bath so hot, the bathroom filled with steam.

She left the comfort of the water only when it began to cool and she'd nearly fallen asleep. Dressing in a royal-blue velour pants suit, she went down to the kitchen where Charlie was sitting with a cup of coffee and the newspaper on the table in front of him. He was absently stroking Benjamin who was curled in his lap and looking quite content. Man and feline looked up as she entered the room. Charlie pushed himself to his feet, causing a disappointed cat to jump to the floor before leaping back onto the seat's warm cushion.

"I thought you might like some hot soup after your bath," he said, pulling out a chair for her. "Sit and I'll get a bowl for you." Going to a pot on the stove, he said over his shoulder, "I hope you don't mind, but I rummaged around in your fridge and pretty much made myself at home."

As he ladled soup into two bowls, Edna said to his back, "If Starling is ever mean to you, you just let me know."

They both laughed as he placed the soup on the table and went back for a cozy-covered teapot. "Made some tea, too," he said, obviously pleased to be serving her. As he sat across the table in a chair next to the one Benjamin had confiscated, he filled her in on what she'd missed when she'd been upstairs. "Carol flew in from Chicago this morning. She saw us drive in and came over to get the Kia. I've shoveled the walks and cleaned off your car, but I still have Santa Claus to get off the roof." He stopped talking then and concentrated too deeply on stirring his soup.

Her heart skipped a beat as she felt something

was wrong. "What is it, Charlie?" she asked, putting down her spoon and staring at him until he met her gaze.

"Starling phoned." He paused, not smiling and barely looking at her.

Edna waited, holding her breath.

"The good news is, they've gotten a flight out from Denver."

The pressure in her chest eased slightly before she asked, "Is there bad news?"

"It isn't until tomorrow. They land in Providence late tomorrow afternoon."

Not trusting herself to say much, Edna pushed her bowl away. Excusing herself, she told Charlie to leave the dishes. She'd clean up later. Right now, she wanted to go upstairs and take a nap.

He watched her with sad eyes. "Will you be okay?" When she merely nodded, he said, "If you're going to lie down, I'll go check on Mary. See if there's anything I can do for her." Ignoring Edna's earlier comment to leave the dishes, he cleared the table and began to load the dishwasher. Twisting to look over his shoulder, he pointed at the wall clock with his chin. "The open house starts in two hours. I'll be back at four to drive you over. Snow's too deep for you to walk."

"Two hours?" She glanced up and gasped. "Is it two o'clock already?" Before he could answer, the phone rang. She picked up the kitchen receiver, saying "Hello" instead of her typical, cheerful "Merry Christmas."

"Merry Christmas, Mother," Matthew Davies greeted in return.

"Merry Christmas, dear." Edna heard the tiredness in her voice, but her eldest child didn't seem to notice.

"I wanted to let you know so you wouldn't worry--Irene and I will be late getting to Mary's this afternoon. Allison and Amanda were invited to a skating party and won't be home until four. We'll be there, but we'll be late."

Edna wasn't happy about the apparent change in her family's plans. She'd been counting on everyone meeting at Mary's on time, but she didn't want to spoil the holiday by arguing. Nothing to be done. "Okay, dear, I'll let her know," was all Edna said before hanging up.

In her bedroom, she set the alarm so she would sleep for no more than an hour. The news that her two youngest children wouldn't be home until late on Christmas Day, plus the news that her other son would be late to the party, kept her from getting much sleep, however. When she finally arose, moving with lead feet and a heavy heart, she showered and dressed. She had expected to begin this year's Christmas celebration with the party next door and her entire family gathered for the first time in three years. Mary had also become part of the family and would join them for Christmas dinner--a dinner that now would be delayed and probably only half enjoyed by the weary travelers.

At 3:52 by the clock on the stove, Edna was standing at the kitchen window, watching for Charlie when the phone rang. She picked up the kitchen receiver instead of going to the office to read the caller-id display.

"Hi, Mother. It's me. Diane."

"Hello, dear. Are you at Mary's?"

"Not yet. I called to say we're running a little late. Roger and Buddy are helping Father into his boots now. We won't be there for another forty-five minutes, at least, but it's an open house, right? No real rush to get there on the dot."

"You're right, dear. No real rush. See you when you get here." Nothing was going the way Edna had hoped. Before she could sink deeper into doldrums, she spotted Charlie's car rounding the driveway. It was precisely four o'clock.

They went in the back door of Mary's house, leaving their coats on the wall pegs. Edna exchanged her faux-fur lined snow boots for silver evening shoes. Mary was waiting impatiently in the door to the kitchen, holding up a cell phone. As soon as Edna recognized her own mobile, Mary laid it on the counter beside the door.

"Don't forget to take it home with you," she said, taking Edna's arm as she drew close.

Arm-in-arm, they passed the archway to the dining room where Edna saw Codfish with his head bent toward Gran. Vinnie was helping Bethany fill a plate from the array of food on Mary's long table. Other guests were milling around, but before Edna could stop to greet them, Mary pulled her forward.

"Come on. You can say hello later. First, everyone who arrives needs to have a picture taken by the tree, before they spill something on their party clothes."

As Edna entered the foyer, she saw a number of people posed on the winding staircase. They were all dressed in red with white trim, and everyone was smiling at her. Mary's ten-foot Christmas tree in the curve of the stairwell was beautifully decorated and twinkling merrily with tiny lights. A man dressed in a green suit coat sat in a wheelchair near the tree, one leg extended.

*He looks like Albert*, she thought. *And that pretty young woman standing next to him could be Starling's double.*

When realization struck, Edna gasped and began to study the faces of the people lining the staircase. They were her children and grandchildren. There was Matthew with his wife Irene and their four children, all grinning broadly. Diane lifted a hand to her shoulder and waggled her fingers. She was standing beside Roger on the stair above Buddy. Grant … was it Grant holding baby Dean? He was one tread higher than Diane, and his wife Karissa was on the stair above him, one hand on his shoulder and the other around their daughter Jillian. Everyone sported Santa hats, even the baby.

"Surprise," they shouted in unison as Edna, dressed in a long, shimmering silver gown, walked slowly into the room, examining each face. She pressed her fingernails hard into her palms. She wouldn't cry. That would fog her vision and ruin an otherwise lovely family photograph.

Carol James, their award-winning photojournalist neighbor, appeared beside Edna, camera in hand. On her other side, Mary said, "The chair beside Albert is for you. Before you start kissing everyone and ruining your lipstick, Carol's going to take some pictures."

And that's what she did. Edna sat beside Albert and kissed his cheek as Carol shot the first photo. When Edna had seen at least half a dozen flashes, she finally waved her arms, stood up and said, "Enough. I want hugs from my family." Turning to face them, she laughed and hugged and kissed and asked, "When did you get here?" to Starling and Grant, and "I thought you were going to be late" to Matthew and Diane.

Matthew said, "It was Mary's idea. She told us we had to get here early. Even Grant arrived with his entourage at three o'clock this afternoon. Good thing Mary has plenty of rooms. We're all staying here tonight."

When Edna had greeted everyone except her granddaughters, nine-year-old Jillian came forward cradling an all-white half-grown kitten in her arms. Beside her, Matthew's youngest child Amanda, who was the same age as Jillian, held Charcoal, while her sister Allison, three years older, had Auntie Bea resting against her shoulder.

"Where in the world …" Edna began kissing each of her granddaughters on the top of her head so as not to crush the cats.

"I adopted 'em," Mary said, coming to stand beside Edna and looking pleased with herself. "I couldn't stand to think of them in that kennel, all alone for Christmas. I phoned Juliana and asked her. The other cat and the two dogs were well enough to go to their homes. That left only these three. Vinnie and Bethany stopped at the clinic on their way here. Hank and Spot have playmates now, but until they all get to know each other better, my two are shut in my rooms."

Edna laughed. "I can see that Hank will have his hands full … or his paws, I should say." She glowered in good humor at Mary. "I think I have a bone to pick with you, my friend."

Mary's wide smile spelled "guilty" all over her face. "I only took the phone out of your bag because I didn't want you calling anyone. Not everyone in your family can keep a secret as well as I can, and I didn't want someone to spoil things."

Just then, Starling walked up to hug her mother. "Sorry if we worried you, Mom. We were under strict instructions not to talk to you. Were you surprised?"

"Was I ever." Edna looked around, but Mary had gone off to the dining room, as had everyone else except Albert. "Wait until I get my hands on her," Edna said. "And you …" She shook a finger playfully at Charlie as he came into the room and pretended to hide behind Starling. "I didn't know you could fib so well."

He laughed and bent forward to kiss her cheek. "Job training," he said.

"Well, you two had better go get some food before those teenage boys eat it all," she said, referring to Matthew's two sons, seventeen-year-old Joey and fifteen-year-old David who had vanished into the kitchen with Diane's Buddy, while the girls played with the cats.

When they were finally alone in the room, Edna sank into the chair beside Albert. "Merry Christmas, dear."

He put an arm around her shoulders, pulled her

close and kissed her temple. "Merry Christmas, sweetheart." Drawing back slightly, he looked into her eyes. "While I was being pampered by Diane, did you get through everything on your list?"

"Nearly everything," she said, being purposely vague. She was trying not to think of the past five days or how close they'd come to a disastrous Christmas.

"Even the cards?" he asked, eyes widening in mock surprise and admiration.

"We're sending valentines this year," she said, giving him a peck on the cheek.

# # #

## Acknowledgements

A special "thank you" to Susie Bowers for sharing her fractured-kneecap experience with me and to Jim Bowers for follow-up care advice.

I believe nobody knows more about cat lore and behavior than Kris Field (BarnwaterCats.org), an amazing defender of felines and a dedicated rescuer of displaced and abused animals of all species. Thank you for all you've taught me and all you do, Kris.

As always, I am indebted to Jan Reynolds, Gail Lindsey, Lori Gee, Jim Coleman and Olivia Coleman for their time, expertise and feedback as first readers.

I especially wish to acknowledge my critique group partner Bonnie McCune (BonnieMcCune.com) who has stayed with me since 2000, generously sharing her support, guidance and insights. You're the best, Bonnie!

Last, but certainly not least, to all my family, friends and readers who have been so supportive and encouraging, you make my efforts fun and rewarding. Many thanks!

## About the Author

Suzanne Young was born and raised in Rhode Island. She has worked as a photographer, a writer, an editor, and a computer analyst since earning her degree in English from the University of Rhode Island in Kingston.

A resident of Colorado for over 40 years, she retired from software development in 2010 to write fiction full time.

She is a member of Denver Woman's Press Club, Rocky Mountain Fiction Writers and Sisters in Crime as well as a graduate of the Arvada (CO) Citizens Police Academy.

To learn more about this author, she invites you to visit her website at www.SuzanneYoungBooks.com where you can also contact her via e-mail.